Wanda
the
Worrywart

Wanda the Worrywart

Mary Towne

ATHENEUM   1989   NEW YORK

Atheneum
Macmillan Publishing Company
866 Third Avenue, New York, NY 10022
Collier Macmillan Canada, Inc.
First Edition
Printed in the United States of America
Designed by Kimberly M. Hauck

10 9 8 7 6 5 4 3 2 1

Library of Congress Cataloging-in-Publication Data
Towne, Mary.
Wanda the worrywart/Mary Towne.
—1st ed. p. cm.
Summary: Wanda's worries become even greater than usual during her
family's summer vacation at a Vermont lodge when her divorced
stepgrandmother develops an interest in a prospective new husband.
ISBN 0–689–31511–2
[1. Vacations—Fiction. 2. Grandmothers—Fiction.] I. Title.
PZ7.T6495Wan 1989
[Fic]—dc20 89–6672 CIP AC

Author's note:

Potter's Lodge is loosely based on Quimby Country, a family resort in Vermont's Northeast Kingdom. No resemblance is intended between my characters and actual guests or staff members at Quimby's. I have also taken a good many liberties as to details of setting and accommodation.

Chapter 1

FOR MOST OF THE LONG DRIVE up to Vermont, Wanda had been worried about getting carsick. Not that she usually did; but then she didn't usually have to sit crammed between her little brother, who smelled (not unpleasantly) of bubble gum, and a person drenched in perfume, hair spray, and bug repellent, who also took up more than her fair share of room. The bug repellent was in case a mosquito should somehow be siphoned into the car through the inch of open window that was all Phyllis would allow on her side, even before the air-conditioning was turned on. Phyllis was allergic to insect bites.

During the last hour or so, though, Wanda's main worry had been about running out of gas. She'd seen her father hesitate when they came to what she knew was the last gas station before the pumps at the country store near the turnoff for Potter's, still miles and miles away, up near the Canadian border. Then he'd pressed his foot down again and driven on. By craning her neck and bracing herself against the vanity case Phyllis kept wedged between them on the seat, Wanda had been able to see that the gauge read half empty. Half empty! The fact that an optimist would have said it was half full was of small comfort to Wanda.

Her father didn't stop at Marie's, either, when they finally got there, but that was okay—if they ran out of gas now, it wouldn't be all that far to walk. Wanda relaxed as they headed down the familiar dirt road, green summer woods filling the windows on either side of the car. Then she realized she needed to go to the bathroom. Immediately the road seemed endless, especially the last part alongside the lake, with the car barely moving and Andrew bouncing up and down beside her, yelling things like, "I see the archery place! I see the badminton net, and the swings, and the tennis court! I see the porch!"

Up on the broad veranda that ran around two sides of Potter's Lodge, Steve was the first to spot the new arrivals. "Here come the Munsons," he announced in his confident way.

"Where?"

His sister Angie abandoned her search for a badminton racket that still had all its strings, and went to join him at the railing. All she could see was a distant cloud of beige dust marking the approach of a car along the dirt road that led in to Heron Lake from the state highway a mile away. "You can't see that far," she accused.

"No, dummy, but I looked at the blackboard in the office, and that's who's supposed to be coming today. 'Willard and Florence Munson,' " Steve quoted. " 'Wanda, Andrew, and Phyllis.' "

"Phyllis? Who's Phyllis? Hey, do you think maybe the Munsons had a baby?" Angie widened her blue eyes; she loved babies, at least to look at.

Steve shrugged. He never offered an opinion on anything he hadn't researched.

"Maybe it's a friend of Wanda's," Sally North said languidly. She was sprawled in one of the big wooden rockers that sat facing out over the lake.

"I don't think Wanda has friends," Angie objected. "Not like that. She's too . . ." But she couldn't think of the word she wanted.

3

"A baby! Boy, that's all we need around here," grumbled her cousin Gus, who was hunkered down on the front steps trying to unpick a length of tangled fishing line. "A person can't get any sleep in this place, anyway, what with the woodpeckers and the bullfrogs and those crazy loons laughing their heads off in the middle of the night. A baby crying will make everything just about perfect."

Gus made this same complaint every year when he first got up to Vermont from New York City, where sirens and buses and early-morning garbage trucks were just so much background noise to him. On the other hand, Gus was a demon fisherman, and there weren't many trout worth catching in the East River.

"At least you're not right next door to the Kirbys and that hyper dog of theirs," Sally told him. "It has a barking fit every time a leaf moves, practically. Of course, it's a city dog," she added slyly.

"I'm surprised you even hear it, the way you sleep," Gus retorted. "I thought your father had to use dynamite to get you out of bed in the morning."

Steve and Angie ignored them, watching the car emerge from behind a feathery screen of birch trees at the far end of the lake. From there the road narrowed and made a straight run in to the lodge between shining water on one side and shady high ground on the other dotted with one- and two-story frame cabins.

Heavy footsteps clumped toward them from the far end of the veranda—Rita Crawford, back from swimming over at the big lake. She had on her purple bathing suit with the gold zigzag in front and the thick-soled hiking boots she always wore, except when she was wearing her cowboy boots for riding. The effect was a little peculiar, but then Rita came from out West somewhere and did things like riding in barrel races and raising calves for 4-H.

She paused in front of the outdoor blackboard and said, "Oh, hey, a hike to Eagle Rim tomorrow. I heard that's a real good climb. You guys gonna go?"

"It's supposed to be for the older kids," Steve told her with a shrug. "The teenagers. And adults, I guess. But you could ask Ray."

Sally said, "How was the water? I was thinking of going swimming, it's so hot. But then I decided I'd just get hot again coming back."

Gus snorted at the idea of Sally's doing anything as strenuous as walking the quarter mile of trail over to Great Harriman, but Rita said seriously, "You wouldn't if you stayed in long enough. It's freezing."

The approaching car had slowed to an obedient crawl as it came to the weathered 15 MPH sign planted in the fireweed opposite the end cabin, but Steve could see now it was a sedate, dark-green Olds with New Jersey plates—the Munsons, sure enough.

Chapter 2

IF ONLY THEY KNEW WHICH CABIN they were going to have, Wanda thought, she could ask to be let off while her father drove on down to the lodge to check in. But Ray never told people that ahead of time; he said he liked to keep things flexible in case of last-minute reservations. Dad said it was more a matter of old plumbing and wiring, and needing to be able to shift people around when something went on the fritz. No one ever made last-minute reservations at Potter's, he pointed out. It never advertised, nor was it on the way to anywhere.

Of course there was a rest room in the lodge itself, but Wanda felt it would be too embarrassing to make a beeline for it the minute she got out of the car—as good as announcing to everyone in sight that she needed to go. And sure enough, there were Angie and Steve up on the veranda, and their cousin Gus (Wanda had a secret crush on Gus, whose scowling dark looks appealed to her), also Sally North and a girl in a purple bathing suit Wanda didn't know, who was sitting astride the railing as if she were riding a horse.

The car slowed even more, easing gingerly over the speed bump by the badminton lawn. Phyllis had the vanity case on her lap now and was squinting into the mirror inside the lid while she applied fresh lipstick to her large, gooey-looking mouth. When they finally stopped, and Mr. Munson opened his door, letting in a wash of warm, sunlit air that smelled of grass and pine and wild mint, she snapped down the lid and said with a frown, "I thought it was always supposed to be so cool up here. Feels like it's as hot as anywhere else."

"Well, usually we get some rain," Wanda's mother said comfortingly—an understatement, since in the three summers the Munsons had been coming to Potter's Lodge, it had rained for at least one week of their two-week vacation. But somehow no one really minded. There were plenty of things you could do when it rained. Besides, the rain made the woods smell good, a smell Wanda sometimes remembered and hugged to herself during slushy, gray February days in New Jersey.

One thing Wanda didn't worry about was whether Phyllis was going to like Potter's and have a nice, relaxing time here, as Mom kept telling her she would. Phyllis was going to hate it, and that was that.

"I wonder what Wanda's going to end up worrying about this year," Steve remarked, watching the oncoming car jounce slowly over the bump in the road next to the badminton lawn. "Remember last year how she kept worrying it would be too cold for the lobster cookout? And about Tommy Hurst falling off the dock into the lake, the way his baby-sitter kept letting him play around down there with the bait cans?"

"Well, it *was* cold at the lobster cookout," Angie pointed out. "It was so freezing, nobody's butter would stay melted in those little cups."

"And Tommy Hurst did fall in the lake," Gus added, with the first smile anyone had seen on his face since that morning, when he'd snagged his line in some lily pads and lost one of his favorite flies. "Mrs. Rowan almost ran over him in her canoe, remember?"

"Sure," Steve said. "But what good did worrying about it do?"

Angie pondered this for a moment. "Well, Wanda was warmer than anyone else at the cookout, because she had her long underwear on. And maybe Tommy wouldn't have been wearing his life jacket if Wanda hadn't always been worrying about him drowning."

Around the corner of the veranda, the screen door to the office flapped open and feathered shut again behind Ray Wallace, who with his wife, Nora, managed Potter's Lodge and Family Camp. Ray paused for a moment to smooth back his hair and tuck his cotton plaid shirt more tidily into his pants. Then, his toothy smile in place, he bounded down the side steps just as the green Olds eased to a stop beside the sloping flower bed that separated the road from the long, graveled path leading back to the cabins.

"Well, now," he cried heartily, flinging his arms wide in welcome, "just look who's here!"

Since all the windows were shut tight, presumably to keep in the air-conditioning, it was several moments before anyone in the car responded to Ray's greeting. Then the driver's door opened, and Mr. Munson got out stiffly.

" 'Lo, there, Ray," he said, and nodded to the kids up on the veranda. "Nice to be back. Where've you put us this year? Not in Tree Swallow, I hope."

All the cabins were named after birds. Tree Swallow was disliked by adults because it had a small porch and no bathroom upstairs, also because it was the cabin nearest the lodge and tended to be noisy, with people going to and fro along the path below. Kids of course liked it for that same reason—because it was close to everything.

"No, no," Ray assured him, opening the passenger door for Mrs. Munson. "I've got you in Kingfisher, with that nice back bedroom for your mother."

"Stepmother, actually," Mr. Munson corrected him, rather grimly. But Ray was beaming his smile now on Mrs. Munson. "Well, now, Florence," he said, helping her out of the car, "you're certainly looking in the pink."

Mrs. Munson gave a flustered giggle. She was wearing a shocking-pink top and matching slacks, and, as Sally North remarked in an undertone to Angie, was someone who never should have worn either slacks *or* pink.

Andrew scrambled out of the back seat, followed more slowly by Wanda. Andrew was plump and roly-poly like his mother, while Wanda had her father's skinny, narrow-shouldered build and limp, mouse-brown hair. But whereas Mr. Munson just looked tired, Wanda's face had a pinched expression, her dark eyebrows drawn together in a little frown of anxiety.

"And this must be the other Mrs. Munson," Ray said enthusiastically, hurrying around the other side of the car to help out the remaining passenger. This was a tall, statuesque woman in a clinging white dress and very high-heeled sandals with glitter on the buckles. She was clasping a blue vanity case to her considerable bosom and had a lot of dark-red hair the same purplish color as the hollyhocks over by the flag-pole. Most of the hair was piled high on top of her head, the rest tumbling down her long white neck in a complicated cascade of little curls and ringlets.

The watchers on the veranda exchanged glances and shrugged. This must be Phyllis—just some kind of grandmother of Wanda's. Not that she looked much like a grandmother. Nor did she look much like the usual Potter's Lodge kind of guest, though maybe she would after she got changed into her old clothes.

"My, just smell the air," the woman said vaguely, in a throaty voice with a flat little edge to it. She slipped on a pair of enormous dark glasses and turned to gaze past the sunbaked clay of the tennis court at the reed-fringed shore of the lake. "Pretty. Except of course the bottom . . . I never could stand mucky bottoms. But never mind, I'll be perfectly happy sunbathing down on that cute little dock where all the boats are."

"Oh, no one swims in Heron Lake," Ray told her hastily, while Mr. Munson frowned at Andrew, who had been overcome with mirth at the mention of mucky bottoms. "We have another lake for swimming, or rather some frontage on it, where there's a nice sandy bottom. . . ."

Now he too frowned at Andrew. "It's just a short hike through the woods," he added, looking a bit doubtfully at Phyllis's shoes. "Well, now, let's get you folks settled. Willard, you want to back the car up? Or maybe it'd be easier to go turn around by the stables. . . . I'll send Pierre along to help with your bags."

"Is Pierre still here?" Wanda spoke for the first time. She looked pleased, or at least as pleased as she ever did. "I thought maybe he'd died," she explained. "Because of being so old, I mean."

Up on the veranda, Steve made a face. "Same old Wanda," he said. "I'll bet Pierre's in better shape than she is."

"She didn't mean she *wanted* him to have died," Angie protested. "Just the opposite."

Pierre was the elderly French Canadian who served as Potter's man-of-all-work. In his younger days he'd been a guide and was said to have Indian blood, though you wouldn't have thought it to look at him—a wiry little man with bright blue eyes, a ready smile, and a bald head tanned the color of a walnut.

"He's always coughing, though," Rita observed. "And sometimes he sort of wheezes, too."

"Because he has a cold," Gus said, glowering at her. He'd been learning some French so he could talk to Pierre better, mainly about fishing. "Anybody can get a cold."

"Yes, don't *you* start doing it," Sally told Rita with her lazy smile.

"Doing what?"

"Worrying."

Chapter 3

ONCE THEY WERE ALL OUT of the car, with Ray fussing around them and Andrew having a fit of giggles about something, Wanda thought maybe the feeling of needing to go to the bathroom would go away, but it didn't. She debated making a dash for Kingfisher on her own, as if she just couldn't wait to explore or start getting settled or something. But it would be a pretty long dash—Kingfisher was one of the rear cabins, set high on the slope way back opposite the archery range.

Now, though, there was a stir of activity around the lodge. The Kirbys came along to play tennis and stopped to greet Wanda's parents, and a new family that had been out in a rowboat trailed up the path from the dock and stood around while Ray introduced them. With no one paying attention to her, Wanda was able to make an unobtrusive getaway, up the side steps and through the empty office to the rest room at the back of the lodge.

This wasn't a real rest room like they had in schools and restaurants, with stalls whose latches might not fasten all the way—or worse, get stuck. It was more like an ordinary house bathroom, with checked curtains at the window and a regular bar of soap in a little flowered dish on the basin. That was the kind of thing Wanda found comforting about Potter's. For a while there'd been a sign on the outside of the door that said "The Facility," but Nora had said it was tacky and made Ray take it down. So now there wasn't any sign—you just had to know where the bathroom was. But that was okay, since Wanda did.

She twitched one of the curtains aside to look out into the sunny yard that separated the kitchen porch from the rambling frame building where the staff lived, except for Ray and Nora, who had their own winterized cabin up behind Tree Swallow. Across the way, beyond the wooden signpost pointing to the Lake Trail and the Ledge, was a long, low structure with a sagging roof that served as a car shed for people whose cabins didn't have driveways or level ground to park on.

One of the stable cats was curled up on a heap of empty lunch knapsacks at the end of the kitchen porch, but you couldn't see the stables themselves from here. Wanda wondered if Karen was back again as riding teacher this year. Well, not teacher exactly, but the person in charge of the horses who checked you out and took you on trail rides. Actually, Karen was a bit casual for Wanda's taste. She always seemed to be talking to someone over her shoulder when she tested your girth, and on the trail she was apt to start a canter without necessarily looking to make sure everyone was really ready, with no overhanging branches in the way.

If Butterscotch was back, too, though, Wanda guessed she might go riding once or twice. The thing about Butterscotch was you didn't have to worry about him doing anything *suddenly,* he was so fat and lazy. In fact, to make him canter at all, you had to kick him hard five or six times and slap him with the reins and sometimes even yell at him. By that time, the others would often have finished their canter and dropped back to a walk, and then all you had to do was trot to catch up with them. (Butterscotch, of course, was always at the end of the line.)

After washing her hands and looking in the mirror to see if the mole above her right eyebrow had changed size or shape since the last time she'd remembered to check it—an early-warning sign of skin cancer, according to a medical program she'd watched on TV—Wanda went along the hall past the office into the main room of the lodge.

As usual at this time of day, the big high-raftered room was almost deserted. An elderly couple was working on the jigsaw puzzle in the corner and a hairy young man in shorts sat reading a newspaper on one of the red-leather benches near the fireplace, but that was all. Through the glass doors into the dining room, Wanda could see Doris, the middle-aged waitress, setting out silverware on a long table for the Saturday-night buffet. There were other waitresses, of course, but they were college girls who changed from year to year; Doris was local and permanent.

As Wanda stood inhaling the familiar smells of woodsmoke and leather and hundreds of books—bookshelves ran all the way around the room, stopping only for doors and windows and the huge, smoke-blackened fireplace—the screen door from the front veranda slapped open, and the girl in the purple bathing suit came in. She planted herself in front of Wanda and said, "You want to play checkers?"

Wanda looked at her. She had reddish-blond hair pulled back into a single thick braid, and wore heavy hiking boots that looked too big for her long, pale legs. She shook her head. "We just got here."

"Yeah, I know. Your family was looking for you. You're Wanda, right? I told them you were in the john. They went to unload the car, all except that tall lady that's all dressed up. She lost her earring over by the tennis court. Steve and Angie and those guys are helping her look for it."

"Phyllis," Wanda said with a sigh.

"I guess. She really your grandmother? That's what they said, but she doesn't look old enough to be."

"She's not," Wanda said. "I mean, she's only a stepgrandmother, sort of. She used to be married to my grandfather," she explained, "but they got divorced. He's had two more wives since her. The one before Phyllis was my real grandmother, only she died."

"So this Phyllis isn't even any relation?" The girl stared. "Then how come she lives with you?"

"She doesn't," Wanda said, and hoped fervently that this would turn out to be true. "She's just visiting for the summer. She had to sell her house down in Florida, and now she just visits people, I guess. The ones she was supposed to stay with this summer got sick or something. My grandfather's new wife wouldn't let him give Phyllis any more money," she added, and lowered her voice as the hairy young man looked up at her over the top of his newspaper. Why did everything about Phyllis have to be so embarrassing? "Anyway, that's why she had to sell her house and her car and all her furniture and stuff. And then my mom invited her."

The girl chewed the end of her braid thoughtfully. "Why would your mom do that?"

"I don't know. She felt sorry for her, I guess. She didn't know what Phyllis was like. My dad tried to tell her, but she said he'd only ever met Phyllis about three times—she wasn't married to my grandfather very long, see, and anyway my dad was already grown up by then. Mom said probably Phyllis would have changed. Because of being old and lonely and poor and everything. But Phyllis isn't like that."

"No," the girl agreed. She studied Wanda for a moment, then stuck out her hand and said abruptly, "My name's Rita Crawford."

Wanda held out her own hand, then recoiled. "Ow!" She stared at her fingers, half expecting to see broken bones sticking out of them.

"I always shake hands too hard," Rita said with an air of pride. "My dad says I don't know my own strength. Out in Colorado, where I come from, we do a lot of arm wrestling."

Wanda nodded uncertainly, massaging her knuckles. She was thinking she should probably go back to the cabin now and help unpack. On the other hand, she didn't want to get trapped into helping hunt for Phyllis's earring.

As if reading her thoughts, Rita tromped over to one of the windows and reported, "They still haven't found it. Now the Kirbys are looking, too. Or at least Mr. Kirby is. Mrs. Kirby's just standing there bouncing a ball on her racket. She looks kind of mad. Do you play tennis?"

"A little," said Wanda. She tried to do everything at Potter's at least once each season—even archery, although she always worried about hitting a bird or a squirrel by mistake.

"I don't. Even though I'm very athletic, I hardly ever play games," Rita informed her.

"They don't test you enough. Not like going *against* yourself, know what I mean?"

Wanda didn't, but she didn't like to say so, so she just shrugged. "Is this your first time here?" she asked.

"Yeah. I'm visiting my grandmother—my real grandmother. Mrs. Rowan. You know her?"

Wanda nodded. Everyone knew Mrs. Rowan, who owned her own cabin and was the nearest thing Potter's had to a permanent guest. She arrived in May before the season opened and stayed until after the first frosts in the fall. She'd been a niece of the founder, a millionaire sportsman named Ephraim Potter, who built the lodge back in the early 1900s as his private hunting and fishing camp. Sometimes Mrs. Rowan had friends to stay and gave cocktail parties on her porch, and sometimes she helped Nora with the gardening or ran errands over in Gilead, New Hampshire, the nearest town of any size. Mostly, though, she went bird-watching.

"She's still out on the lake, I guess," Rita said, looking a little wistful. "We were supposed to go up to Marie's for an ice cream this afternoon, but I guess she forgot."

As Wanda knew, Mrs. Rowan was capable of sitting motionless in a canoe or rowboat for hours at a time, her binoculars trained on waterfowl or on land birds among the trees on the far shore or on the great blue herons at the south end that gave the lake its name. Sometimes she'd forget to come back in for dinner, and Nora would have to ring the bell an extra time for her.

It occurred to Wanda that having Mrs. Rowan for a grandmother might be almost as weird at times as having Phyllis for one; not that she actually did, she reminded herself. She also realized whom Rita looked like—old Ephraim Potter himself, whose portrait hung above the fireplace. She had the same color hair and pale eyes and square, aggressive-looking jaw.

"I know," Rita said, following her glance. She scowled. "You might be stuck with Phyllis," she said, "but at least you're not related to a murderer."

"A murderer?" Wanda looked at her wide-eyed.

"All those deer and elk and lions and things. Oh, the lions weren't around here," Rita said as Wanda frowned. "I guess they were in Africa, and the elephants, too. Isn't that gross, killing an elephant? The only thing I'd ever kill would be a rattlesnake, and only if it was all coiled up ready to strike. And wasps, if they bother me. Well, if you don't want to play checkers, I guess I'll go back to the cabin and work on my whittling. I'm making a pipe stand for my dad."

"I'll go with you," Wanda said quickly, on sudden inspiration. "The back way, okay? I should take my mom some vases. She always likes to have a whole bunch of them."

They went out the side door and around to the shelves at the rear corner of the veranda, where Nora kept an assortment of jars and bottles for guests who liked to arrange wildflowers in their cabins. Wanda grabbed a couple of jars at random and headed up toward the cabin path, keeping Rita between herself and the group she could see out of the corner of her eye still milling around on the grass beside the tennis court. Rita was taller than she was, and with any luck Phyllis might not spot her; also Wanda would have the excuse for her mother that she hadn't gone to help Phyllis because she'd been busy making a new friend.

As they turned past Tree Swallow, where the mother of the new family was trying to find room on the porch for things like beach chairs and rain boots and a soccer ball, Rita said, "You like hiking and camping, stuff like that?"

"Sure."

"I mean, you're not scared of skunks or por-cupines or poison mushrooms?"

Skunks? Porcupines? Poison mushrooms? Wanda had never thought of these. What she mainly worried about in the woods—apart from getting lost, of course—was meeting a moose.

"I tried to get that Sally to hike around Heron Lake with me, because you're not supposed to go alone, but she kept saying about all that stuff, and also there might be bears."

"Oh, Sally." Wanda's brow cleared. "She was just making up excuses. Sally hates exercise, she's really lazy. The most she'll ever do is play Ping-Pong, and sometimes badminton for about ten minutes."

"Well, hey, you want to hike around the lake tomorrow? Or no, I guess tomorrow I'm going up to Eagle Rim. That's supposed to be for older kids, but Ray said he thought I was up to it." Rita lengthened her stride importantly past Merganser and Cedar Waxwing. "Maybe the day after."

"Well, I don't know about around the lake," Wanda said cautiously. Not only was that a really long hike, it was also the one place where you actually might meet a moose. At least, a few years ago someone had caught a glimpse of mooselike antlers through the trees at the edge of the south marsh. "We could go up on the Ledge Trail, though, if you want."

"Okay."

Rita stuck out her hand again, but Wanda pretended not to see it. Up ahead, her mother was waving to her from the high front porch of Kingfisher, while her father struggled up the path from the road with what looked like a last load of gear, including Phyllis's special nonallergenic pillows in their pale-blue satin cases.

Chapter 4

AS WANDA HAD EXPECTED, Phyllis managed to complain about almost everything, except she did it in a way you couldn't quite call complaining. This kept Mr. Munson from getting mad at her out loud as Wanda knew he wanted to, and also allowed Mrs. Munson to believe Phyllis was having a wonderful time "getting away from it all." Wanda couldn't think what Phyllis had to get away from, except their house in New Jersey, where she'd spent most of her time reading magazines and watching game shows on TV and calling up her friends in Florida at the Munsons' expense.

As for the simple life Wanda's mother kept sighing happily about while she stuffed goldenrod and fireweed and meadowsweet into old apple-juice bottles, it seemed to Wanda that a complicated life would be more Phyllis's style—one she could have changed her clothes for five or six times a day instead of just the two or three times she did here, from one color-coordinated resort outfit to another. When Mrs. Munson asked mildly if she hadn't brought along some casual clothes like sweatshirts and jeans, Phyllis retorted that she wouldn't be seen dead in a sweatshirt and that she thought jeans looked tacky on older women. Since Mrs. Munson happened to be wearing jeans at the time, Wanda thought maybe that would give her pause; but she just laughed and said oh, she'd long since given up worrying about her appearance, and anyway she'd never had any real fashion sense, not like Phyllis.

Phyllis said it was quaint having just a curtained-off corner in her room instead of a regular closet, and of course Wanda and Andrew wouldn't mind if she hung some of her things in theirs (which was a regular closet, though small). She said it was sweet of Pierre to come start the fire in the wood stove so early in the morning, even if he did make a lot of noise with the dampers and kept whistling the same three notes over and over again between his teeth, whenever he wasn't coughing.

It was too bad about the water pressure, Phyllis said, but never mind, the water tasted delicious, and she could always take a bar of soap with her over to the big lake any time she wanted to feel really clean. Funny the lake water was so cold, though, positively icy; it must be because they were so far north. She kept forgetting that, because of course there weren't any snowcapped mountains around to look at, just these round green hills that all looked the same to her, even if they each had a different name and were called mountains on the map.

Then there was not having any TV, except for one small set in the lodge that got only two channels, neither of them clearly. "Of course, I can see why you wouldn't want one of those ugly big antennas on the roof," she told Nora with a bright little laugh. "And I suppose you're too far from everywhere for cable TV. I mean, it's so rustic here, isn't it?"

"That's us," Nora agreed tersely. "Rustic. You will remember about not using your hair dryer at the same time as the curling wand, won't you, Mrs. Munson?"

This was on their way in to dinner on their second night. That afternoon Phyllis had succeeded in blowing a fuse that knocked out half the electricity in the camp.

"Oh, please just call me Phyllis. Or Mrs. M., if you think that's too informal," Phyllis said graciously—making it clear she disapproved of the way Nora and Ray called everyone by their first names, and vice versa. "I feel so dumb about not reading that little card better, the one that's tacked inside the bathroom door. Of course the typing's all blurry because of the steam . . . but never mind, I'm sure it was all my fault. I never did understand about watts and volts and all that."

"Oh, well, gave us a chance to check out the emergency generator," Ray said easily. "Something we should do from time to time, anyway. No harm done."

"Except possibly to the food," Nora said. "Oh, I don't mean anything's been in danger of spoiling," she added, though Wanda could have sworn she paused deliberately to let Phyllis think about food poisoning for a moment or two. "I was thinking of the cook. Excuse me, I'd better go see if he's in a better mood now."

She moved swiftly away, spare and straight-backed in her no-nonsense shirtdress and cardigan and flat shoes.

"They were so lucky to get Terence back this year," Wanda's mother explained as the Munsons went on into the dining room. "He had

30

lots of other offers, even though he's still only in college or chef's school or whatever it's called. Of course his specialty is pastry," she added, and then looked as if she wished she hadn't.

This was because of Phyllis's remarks about the food. She said home-style cooking was just another term for starch. Phyllis was always talking about her figure and her complexion. At home, Wanda and Andrew had been served more raw vegetables and cottage cheese and granola that summer than they usually saw in a whole year. But Wanda happened to know that Phyllis kept a box of Mallomars under her nightgowns in the bottom drawer of her dresser—the dresser that had been Wanda's until Phyllis came and Wanda had to move in with Andrew. She hadn't told on Phyllis; she wasn't quite sure why. She thought maybe she was saving it.

Today at lunch, while the rest of the family ordered the chicken croquettes and popovers, Phyllis had sat deliberating aloud over the choice of soups on the menu Nora typed up each day. "The creamed corn is probably just that gluey Campbell's stuff," she'd said with a shudder. "And who knows what's in the minestrone."

"The corn soup is made with fresh corn," Doris had said tonelessly, fixing her gaze on her pad and pencil. "And the tomatoes in the minestrone are from my own garden."

"Really?" Phyllis said, in a tone that said she didn't believe a word of it. "I think I'll just have a tossed green salad. You do have something besides iceberg lettuce, I hope?"

"The house dressing?" Doris asked, ignoring this.

"Oh, spare me." Phyllis made a little face. "No, just bring me the oil and vinegar. I'm sure I'll be better off making my own."

Wanda had cringed, but at least there'd been hardly anyone else in the dining room at the time. Most people ordered picnics for lunch or made their own sandwiches if they were in housekeeping cabins. The Munsons themselves were having lunch in the dining room only because it was their first full day, and because of Phyllis.

If Phyllis made a fuss about the food tonight, though, Wanda thought she would die. At the buffet last night, people had sat wherever they wanted or taken their plates out on the veranda, but tonight everyone was at their regular tables. Wanda's heart sank when she saw theirs was next to the long table shared by Gus and his parents with Steve and Angie and theirs. Mrs.

Jacobson and Mrs. Hyatt were sisters, tanned, casual types who tended to dress alike. Tonight they were wearing loose silk shirts and white pants. Wanda saw them lift their eyebrows as Phyllis swished into her chair in a cloud of perfume and an emerald-green chiffon dress with a beaded top and matching earrings.

It wasn't just a question of embarrassment, either. Wanda worried that Terence might quit if Phyllis kept sending her plate back to the kitchen, the way she'd done at the restaurant in New Jersey where they'd gone for Wanda's parents' anniversary. Terence tended to quit several times a season as it was, which meant Nora had to take over the cooking along with all her other work while Ray sweet-talked him back. If Phyllis made him mad enough, though, he might even quit for good.

At least Doris wasn't going to be their waitress again. Maybe she'd asked not to be. The plump blond girl who took their order just nodded meekly when Phyllis asked to have her shrimp cocktail served plain with a lemon wedge on the side and only one thin slice from the end of the roast beef, without gravy.

"Well, now," Mr. Munson said, leaning back in his chair while they waited for their food.

"Everyone in good voice for the sing tonight? I'll be taking my usual turn at the piano, I guess, with Bill Kirby to spell me on the requests. Too much to expect it's been tuned since last year, I suppose."

He spoke dryly, but Wanda thought how her father already looked easier and more relaxed, the way he always did at Potter's, even though he hadn't done much more today than read the Sunday paper on their front porch and take Andrew out in a rowboat for a while. Tomorrow he was going to play golf at a course up in Canada with Dr. North and some other men.

"The sing?" Phyllis suppressed a yawn, toying with the emerald-and-pearl bracelet she wore around one wrist.

"Oh, yes, you'll enjoy that, Phyllis," Mrs. Munson told her.

"Down in the rec house," Mr. Munson explained. "You know the sort of thing—hymns, folk songs, Gilbert and Sullivan, a bit of everything. Good fun usually, and almost everyone turns up for it."

Wanda waited for Phyllis to say "how sweet." Instead she said in a remote voice, "Oh, well, I don't know. . . . I once trained as a professional singer, you know. Everyone said I could have

34

had a career in light opera—my voice wasn't heavy enough for opera, of course—but then I met your dear father, and . . ." She lifted her shoulders in a rueful little shrug.

The way Wanda had heard it, Phyllis had been working as a waitress in some club when her grandfather met her. Of course, maybe she'd been a singing waitress.

"No, I think I'll just have an early night," Phyllis went on, with a sigh. "Go on back to the cabin and read for a while. Of course, that isn't much of a reading light, is it? And I don't suppose I'd dare put a bigger bulb in it."

Her eyes had been wandering as she spoke. Now she sat up straighter in her chair and did something to her shoulders that puffed out her front. Wanda followed her glance. Mr. Farnsworth had just sat down at his small table by the window. He nodded stiffly to several acquaintances, then shook out his napkin and turned his head to look out at the long, evening shadows falling across the lake. In his pale-gray linen jacket and blue silk ascot that picked up the silvery glints in his thick dark hair, he was the dressiest person in the room besides Phyllis.

Andrew had turned in his chair to see who Wanda was looking at. "That's Mr. Farnsworth," he announced. "All he ever does is go fishing. He's mean, too."

"Andrew!" reproved his mother. "He isn't mean, dear, just quiet. And he doesn't like being disturbed when he's fishing, which is only natural."

"Well, he's not quiet then. He *yells* at you."

"Oh, dear." Mrs. Munson faltered; she preferred to believe that everyone in the world was as good-natured as she was. "I don't think Mr. Farnsworth cares much for children," she said finally.

"No," Andrew agreed. "He hates them."

"Has a fine baritone voice, though," Mr. Munson observed. "About the most we ever hear out of him. At the sings, I mean," he explained to Phyllis. "Ought to hear him belting out 'The Battle Hymn of the Republic.' And 'Give Me Some Men Who Are Stouthearted Men'—now there's a good light-opera tune for you—"

The waitress was serving their first courses. Wanda noticed that Phyllis's shrimp cocktail had a lot of tomato sauce on it and only a thin slice of lemon on the side. She waited for Phyllis to say something sharp to the waitress and send it back. But Phyllis started eating as if she hadn't noticed.

"Maybe I'll come along to the sing for a little while, after all," she said casually. "If it's the thing to do—and I certainly don't want to seem standoffish. . . . Is Mr. Farnsworth here on his own, then? I mean, this is such a family-oriented place," she said with distaste. "Perhaps he's a widower? Or divorced?"

Mr. Munson laughed. "Drew Farnsworth? Far as I know, the only thing he's ever been married to is his fishing rod. And I suppose his business. Inherited some kind of optics company, and I gather he's done a good deal of development and expansion over the years. Into weaponry systems now, I believe."

Wanda thought that weaponry systems were just what she would have expected Mr. Farnsworth to be into. She also thought that Mr. Farnsworth was the first thing about Potter's Lodge and Family Camp that had really engaged Phyllis's attention.

Wanda's father was looking thoughtful, as if maybe the same thing had occurred to him. His eyes met Wanda's before he bent over his plate again, and Wanda could tell by the little gleam in them that he was taking the idea a step further, just as she was. Wanda didn't know why she hadn't thought of it before, but of course the

very best and surest way to get Phyllis out of
their lives again once and for all—maybe the
only way—would be to find her a new husband
. . . a new, rich husband.

Chapter 5

"HEY, WHAT'RE YOU DOING THAT FOR?"

Rita stood waiting for Wanda at a bend in the trail. Wanda had taken a yellow Magic Marker from her pocket and was coloring a large bright blob on the slender trunk of a birch tree, just at eye level. "I like to make my own blazes," she explained. "For coming back."

"Why? There're plenty of blazes along here already." Rita pointed at a tree nearby that had a red blotch on it made by painting over a hatchet cut.

"Not enough of them," Wanda told her seriously. "Look how far apart they are. What if you went off the trail for a minute to look at something, and when you came back on it farther on, you'd missed a blaze and you couldn't see the next one?"

"So? You'd keep going and there'd be one around the next bend, probably."

Rita was bouncing up and down as she spoke, to keep her muscles from cooling off. "Anyway, I bet Nora doesn't like you putting yellow gunk all over the woods."

"It's the washable kind," Wanda said, marking another tree halfway between the first one and the tree with the red camp blaze. "It comes off when it rains."

"Yeah, well, it looks like it's gonna start raining anytime now," Rita said, peering up at the gray sky through the tall green peaks of the spruce trees. "What happens then, if you're so scared of getting lost?"

"Oh, I probably wouldn't get lost *here*," Wanda said. "I've been up on the Ledge lots of times. The blazes are just in case. Anyway, it's not going to rain for a while yet." Wanda was a devoted student of the weather and was usually right about it. "If you do get lost, though," she went on earnestly, as Rita stared at her, "you should always make for high ground. Or if there isn't any, or there are so many trees you can't see anything, you should follow a source of water downhill."

Rita shook her head as she turned away. "I guess I'm lucky I have a good sense of direction," she said, and tramped off along the trail.

Wanda followed more slowly, pausing to make a big yellow *X* on a granite outcropping. This was a part of the Ledge trail she didn't care for much; it was sort of dark from all the big rocks and the cedars and spruces, with hardly any wildflowers or berries to add color, in fact, hardly any undergrowth at all, except ferns. Not that Rita would have slowed down to look at a flower, anyway. During the pretty, leafy first part of the trail, she'd marched past a whole little cluster of Indian pipes without a second glance.

"Wanda?"

Rita was having to wait for her again, up ahead where the trail curved around a giant boulder. Wanda quickened her steps apologetically, then found she'd snagged the strap of her canteen on a branch and had to stop to untangle it.

"What do you need that canteen for, anyway?" Rita said. "It isn't even hot. Besides, drinking a lot of water isn't good for you when you're exercising. Except if you're running in a marathon, I guess," she added.

"Oh, I'd never go on a hike without bringing water," Wanda said, aghast at the thought.

"What if you got lost, or fell down and hurt yourself, or got trapped by a forest fire or something, and it might be days before anyone found you? You can live without food for a whole long time—I forget how many days, but it's quite a lot—only you have to have water. I read that in a survival manual, and it was on TV, too."

"But the lake's right down there," Rita said, pointing through the trees. "I mean, you want water, you've got that whole big lake to drink."

"Yeah, but if you were hurt, like if your *leg* was broken—" Wanda shrugged, without finishing her sentence; the point seemed obvious to her.

Rita stared at her for a long moment, her fists on her hips. She wore a green T-shirt and khaki shorts, with a leather belt to which she'd attached her Swiss army knife, also her stopwatch in case she felt like doing wind sprints.

Wanda, by contrast, was wearing jeans and a long-sleeved shirt as protection against deer-flies, briers, poison ivy, poison sumac, and sunburn (in case she was wrong about the weather). She also had a red nylon windbreaker tied around her waist, whose zippered pockets held her first-aid supplies, a compass, a small flashlight with extra batteries, a box of safety matches, a collapsible cup, and some concentrated food in the form of a few Fig Newtons in a plastic bag. The red, of course, was so hunters wouldn't shoot her by mistake. Never mind that it wasn't the hunting season and that, anyway, the woods were posted—Wanda believed you couldn't be too careful.

"I guess those guys were right about you," Rita said finally, with a sigh. "You really do worry a lot, you know, Wanda? In fact, I never met anybody that worried about the kind of stuff you do. And, like, that's okay with me. I think everybody should do their own thing—but it takes a whole lot of *time,* know what I mean? And right now . . ." She looked down, playing with the tail of her braid. "Well, see, I really like to keep moving when I'm out on the trail. So I guess maybe it'd be better if we split up. Sort of both go at our own pace, you know?"

Wanda nodded unhappily, without surprise. She'd known this would come up sooner or later; it always did.

"Like there's probably other stuff we can do together where it won't matter so much," Rita said, looking at Wanda anxiously. When Wanda didn't answer, Rita flipped the tail of her braid back over her shoulder, said, "Well, see you later," and strode away out of sight, her boots clacking against the loose stones on the trail.

Left alone, Wanda made a few more yellow blazes, but in a halfhearted way. Finally she stuffed the Magic Marker back in her pocket and sat down on a big, tilted rock half-carpeted in moss. Actually, she didn't mind being by herself in the quiet woods as long as she knew exactly where she was. (Here Wanda checked the lichen on the surrounding rocks and trees to make sure north was where she thought it should be.) If she sat here long enough, she might see a deer, maybe even a deer with a fawn, and that would really be a whole lot more interesting than trying to keep up with Rita as she rushed through the woods without looking to left or right.

Above her a red squirrel frisked in the branches of a pine, but Wanda didn't raise her head. She studied her sneaker tips for a while, then transferred her gaze to a cluster of colorful funguses growing in a little hollow below the trail. There were big frilly caps and tiny neat ones, in pretty shades of orange and cream and amber and red. She thought about the terrarium she made every year at Potter's to keep on her desk at home, until she forgot to water it and everything inside shriveled up and died. Could you have toadstools in a terrarium? You wouldn't be able to transplant them exactly, but maybe if you dug up a big chunk of the dirt they were growing in. . . .

Of course a lot of them were really poisonous, but that was only to eat, not touch—wasn't it? Wanda thought uncertainly of Sally North's warning to Rita about poison mushrooms. But probably that was just kidding, and anyway it wouldn't matter, because when Wanda collected for her terrarium, she always wore a pair of her mother's rubber gloves.

Wanda realized she'd been hearing voices coming along the trail from the direction of Potter's. Now they were suddenly closer and louder.

"Hey, look!" She recognized Steve's voice and his loud, confident laugh. "Old Wanda must be around here somewhere. Boy, I wish I had my own Magic Marker, or some yellow paint or something. Wouldn't it be great to blaze up a whole wrong trail for her, so she'd wind up going around in circles?"

The second voice said something Wanda couldn't hear, but she could tell it belonged to Gus. The sounds faded as a damp breeze rustled the treetops.

Wanda had been telling herself she didn't care about what Rita had said, but now her eyes stung, and there was a sharp, hard lump in her throat, as if she'd swallowed a peach pit by mistake (something Wanda would never actually do, since whenever she ate a peach she cut it in half first and dug out the pit).

She knew she worried too much, but she couldn't help it—that was just the way she was. Anyway, it seemed to her that *someone* had to worry about things, if only to try and keep them from happening; and then to be prepared if they did anyway. Her father tried to tease her sometimes by saying she was like Atlas, taking the weight of the world on her shoulders. Wanda thought of it more as being a kind of lookout or scout—the person who stayed on duty, so to speak, while others sleepwalked through life or went barging carelessly around, trusting to luck.

Wanda had been thinking the boys must have turned back or taken a side trail. But the big granite outcropping must just have masked the sounds of their approach, because suddenly here they were, emerging into the little clearing where Wanda sat, with Steve in the lead. "Well, what do you know?" he said, slowing to a stop and turning to grin at Gus.

Gus frowned at him. "Hi, Wanda," he said gruffly.

Wanda saw Steve realize she must have heard him making fun of her. His ears turned red. "We're going down to get some frogs in a place Gus knows on Great Harriman," he said casually, running a hand through his short blond hair. "You know—for the contest tomorrow. You want to come?"

The frog-jumping contest was an annual event at Potter's, held on a shady section of the dirt road next to the badminton court. Wanda saw that Gus was carrying a plastic cooler with some holes punched in the top—also that he was scowling in a way that meant Steve shouldn't have asked her.

Before Steve could change his mind, she said quickly, "Sure."

"Usually I just get mine from Heron Lake," Steve explained, "but Gus says he thinks the frogs over here are livelier. Also they're not as used to having people around, so maybe they'll be easier to catch. What are you doing?"

Wanda was carefully stripping some big pieces of moss off the rock she'd been sitting on. "Here," she said, handing them to Gus to put in the cooler. "We can soak them in water, and that'll help keep the frogs from drying out. Sort of like wall-to-wall carpeting, only wet."

Steve laughed, and Gus almost smiled. Wanda hadn't meant to make a joke, just a practical suggestion, but if they thought it was funny, that was okay with her. Pleased with herself, she snugged her jacket more closely around her waist and followed the boys along the trail a short distance to where it made a fork. They took the lower branch downhill through thickets of wild laurel and azaleas, the trail getting narrower and steeper and muddier as they approached the lake. Gus said something about a shortcut and plunged off the trail to scramble down to the shore, grabbing at roots and saplings to keep from slipping on the damp leaves.

"Oh, come *on*," Steve said as Wanda paused and took her Magic Marker out of her pocket. "Wanda, we're not going to get lost here, for Pete's sake! The lake's only about ten yards away."

"I know," Wanda said, marking the tree nearest the edge of the trail. "This is just so when we bring the frogs back, we'll be sure to come to the right place. After the contest, I mean." She remembered about the rain and got out her other marker, the permanent one she always carried along, too.

"Who said anything about bringing them back? We'll just let them go in Heron Lake. Let 'em meet all their distant froggy friends and relations." Steve laughed.

"That wouldn't be right," Wanda objected. "I mean, it's okay to *borrow* them, but when we're through, we should bring them back to their home."

Steve looked at her in exasperation, then sighed. "Okay, but Gus can bring them back by boat when he goes fishing. He's always fishing along this part of the shore. He can just dump 'em in as he goes by." He slithered down the bank to join Gus.

Stubbornly Wanda marked another tree.

Gus was looking thoughtfully at the muddy stretch of shoreline, where small waves lapped at a big flat rock just offshore. "All these little coves look sort of the same from a boat, though," he said. "I guess Wanda's right. If we're going to bring the frogs back at all, we should try and make sure it's the exact same place."

Thrilled by Gus's support, Wanda said recklessly, "You don't even have to bring them if you don't want—I will."

"You won't like carrying them," Steve told her. "Not the way they flip around inside."

This turned out to be true. Although Wanda proved to be the best of the three of them at catching frogs, her hands deft and quick, she decided to let hers go when she saw the way they acted inside the cooler. "I wouldn't want mine to get hurt," she said. "I mean, what if one of the others kicked him in the eye and he went blind or something?"

Steve groaned. "There she goes again—'what if?' I mean, who worries about a *frog*?"

"I do," said Wanda.

"Well, let me have yours, then. He's bigger than mine, and his legs are longer."

But it was too late. Wanda had already dropped her frog back into the lake with a splash.

"How come you didn't mind the catching part?" Gus asked curiously as they headed back along the shore trail, going the long way around by the swimming and picnic area. "I mean, a lot of people won't even *touch* a frog, the way they're all green and slimy and sort of gross. Girls especially."

Wanda looked at him blankly. "But frogs can't do anything to you. I mean, they can't bite you or sting you or anything." She thought for a moment and added, "People used to think you got warts from them, but that's not true. My little brother had warts, and the doctor said they came from a virus. They're catching, but only from other people, not frogs."

50

"Warts!" Behind them, Steve let out a guffaw. "Boy, Andrew better watch out. I mean, never mind a virus, he could catch a worrywart right in his own family." He was so entertained by this witticism he almost fell into the lake. "Worrywarts—get it?" he said, when Gus didn't laugh.

"I got it," Gus said, and turned to glower at him.

Wanda decided Gus had the nicest glower she'd ever seen, nicer than most people's smiles.

Chapter 6

USUALLY PHYLLIS TOOK A LONG NAP in her room after lunch, with both the shades and the curtains drawn and a sleep mask over her eyes. She complained that one of the shades had a hole in it and the curtains didn't meet in the middle, also that the little kids playing on the swing set way down across the road ought to be taking naps, too, instead of making so much noise.

So Wanda was surprised to see her among the adults gathered to watch the frog-jumping contest next day, most of them sitting on plastic garden chairs they'd carried along from the lawn by the tennis court. Then she saw who was sitting next to Phyllis and stopped being surprised—Mr. Farnsworth. He had a pad and pencil on his knee, and from the way he and Phyllis were putting their heads together and whispering and pointing, it looked as if they were planning to bet on the frogs.

At first it had seemed Phyllis wasn't going to get anywhere with Mr. Farnsworth. Mr. Munson had made a point of introducing them before the sing, but although Mr. Farnsworth had nodded politely enough and then looked hard at Phyllis for a moment, the way Wanda had noticed men sometimes did, he'd gone on to take his usual chair at the back of the room and had left right after the sing was over.

Not that he could have helped noticing Phyllis during the sing—no one could have, after she decided to get into the spirit of things. When Mr. Kirby replaced Mr. Munson at the piano to take requests (he could play by ear, which Mr. Munson couldn't), Phyllis kept asking for show tunes that no one else knew all the words to. This meant she was practically singing a solo each time, in a voice that swooped and tacked and fluttered like a kite in a high wind, making Wanda feel vaguely seasick. Even worse, she got up and did an actual solo toward the end, when Mr. Kirby was playing from the Gilbert and Sullivan book (luckily most of the kids had left by then), mincing and smiling and flapping her false eyelashes while she pretended to be someone called Little Buttercup. It was sickening. Wanda could only hope that Mr. Farnsworth was looking out the window and thinking about fish while all this was going on.

Anyway, it didn't look as if Phyllis and Mr. Farnsworth were going to be making beautiful music together, as Wanda's father whispered to her wryly afterward. But then, last night at bingo, they'd discovered they had another mutual interest: fooling around with money.

Mr. Munson said this wasn't necessarily the same thing as gambling in order to *make* money. "Though it probably helped that they sucked in old Mr. Jeffries for a while," he added a bit grimly.

"Sucked him into what?"

Mr. Jeffries was a quavery old man who spent a week at Potter's each year, accompanied by a nurse and an elderly schnauzer dog named Fritz, whom he rather resembled. Wanda remembered he'd been at the same end of one of the long tables as Mr. Farnsworth and Phyllis.

"Side bets," Mr. Munson said. He tried to explain what these were, but math wasn't Wanda's best subject, and besides, she didn't see why anyone would want to bother with anything extra when they were playing bingo. She herself needed all her concentration just to make sure she got the numbers right as Ray called them out. One of the most embarrassing moments of her life so far had been calling out, "Bingo!" and then finding she'd made a mistake about one of the numbers, a G5 that should have been a G9.

But anyway it seemed the betting was what had put Mr. Farnsworth in such a good mood. Usually he just sat brooding over his three cards, the most you were allowed to play at once, at a nickel apiece. But after Phyllis maneuvered herself into an empty chair next to him—making her main move when a bunch of the younger kids were sent off to bed—he became almost animated. By the end of the evening he was talking and smiling more than Wanda had ever seen him do. Since neither he nor Phyllis held a winning card the whole time, Wanda had been puzzled by the little stack of change they kept pushing around between them, also by the notes Mr. Farnsworth kept making on a piece of paper.

Now he was doing the same thing again, only with frogs instead of numbers. Wanda was glad to see that old Mr. Jeffries was nowhere around.

"I don't really approve of that, do you?" Wanda heard one woman say to another. "After all, betting . . . it's supposed to be just good clean fun for the kids."

"Oh, I don't know," the other woman said, and laughed. "She does look as if she were settling down to watch the Kentucky Derby at the very least, doesn't she? I mean, the dark glasses and that *hat*."

Wanda winced. Phyllis was wearing a floaty lavender dress with white edging around the neck and sleeves, and a big, floppy sunhat with a kind of lavender veil thing that tied under her chin. Most of the other women were in pants or shorts, some with raincoats over their shoulders. After a brilliant sunny morning, the sky had clouded over again.

"Do you think Andrew's frog has a chance?" Mrs. Munson asked anxiously, watching Andrew kneel down behind the starting line drawn in the dirt with a small, sleepy-looking frog clutched in his grubby hands. So many kids had entered the contest this year that Ray'd had to divide them into three heats, with a jump-off to follow.

Wanda shook her head. "He's been feeding it too much and playing with it. Treating it like a a pet," she explained, "instead of like a racing frog."

"A pet? Oh, dear, I hope he isn't planning on keeping it."

"No, I'm making him take it back where we got it from, across the lake."

Wanda had decided not to enter the contest herself, but she'd rowed Andrew across Heron Lake that morning to a place where she liked to go collecting for her terrarium. While they were there, he'd managed to capture a little brown-spotted frog, whom he named Buster and carried back in one of his socks.

Secretly Wanda was hoping Gus's frog would win, but it didn't even get into the finals. It squirted off sideways onto the badminton lawn, where it made the most spectacular leap of the day, right up and over the net. Steve's frog won its heat but got turned around and went the wrong way in the finals, bounding fast and straight toward the lodge instead of on down the road. It was Sally North's frog that won, which didn't seem fair. Sally hadn't even caught it herself—Mr. Kirby had rescued it from his dog in the reeds down below the rec house and given it to Sally, who happened to be nearby at the time.

Mr. Farnsworth must have bet on Sally's frog, though, because he looked pleased as he stood up and pocketed a couple of bills Phyllis took from her handbag with much pouting and head-shaking. Then he glanced up at the sky, said it looked like rain again, and went off to collect his fishing gear.

Wanda rowed Andrew back across Heron Lake to the waterlogged tree trunk where he'd found his frog, hoping he wouldn't make a big drama out of letting it go. He didn't. He said, "See you next year, Buster," and told Wanda seriously he thought Buster would have a better chance of winning when he was a year older and had his full growth.

To Wanda's surprise, Phyllis was waiting for them on the dock when they got back, teetering in her high heels on the narrow planks. Wanda exchanged a frowning glance with Andrew; they'd thought Phyllis would be taking her delayed nap by now. She'd removed her dark glasses but still wore the hat.

"Oh, Wanda, dear," she said sweetly, as Wanda shipped the oars and let the boat bump up against the old tires lining the dock, "I wonder if you'd mind taking me for a little spin on the lake. You know, I haven't even been out on the water yet—isn't that silly?" She offered a hand to Andrew, who ignored it and clambered out of the bow on his own. "Somehow I never did learn to row a boat, in spite of all the years I spent at sea, so to speak, with dear Edgar on the yacht."

Edgar was Wanda's grandfather. Wanda's information was that Phyllis had been married to him for about a year and a half.

"Of course we had the dear little dinghy, but usually there was a crew member to row us. And then make himself scarce, of course. Those lovely secluded little coves down in the Caribbean, so romantic . . . not that I'd expect you to understand about that," Phyllis added in her normal, rather raspy voice, as though suddenly remembering it was just Wanda she was talking to.

Wanda shrugged. She enjoyed rowing, and if she refused, her mom would get to hear about it and look at her reproachfully. "Okay. You better take off your shoes, though. There's quite a lot of water in the bottom."

"Oh, well, then I can bail and make myself useful, can't I?" Phyllis said merrily.

She took off her shoes and looked around for a place to put them that wasn't muddy or cluttered with bait cans and mooring lines. Finally she hung them by their straps from an overhanging alder branch, and her handbag, too. Wanda steadied the boat against the dock while Phyllis stepped down into it gingerly and settled herself and her lavender skirts on the stern seat. She noticed Phyllis made no move toward the bailing can.

As they started away from the dock, Phyllis looked around and said brightly, "Well, now, I guess I should go take a look at those big herons everyone's always talking about. Down at that end, are they?"

Obediently Wanda pulled on her right oar and back-watered with her left, pointing the bow south. After about a hundred yards, though, she stopped rowing and said, "I don't like to go any farther than this because of all the water lilies. They get all tangled around the oars, and it's hard to row over them. Especially with the extra weight. But anyway you can see the herons from here, if they're out."

Fishing among the reeds, she meant, where you could sometimes see the big birds standing motionless for minutes at a time, ghostly gray-blue shapes against the vivid green of the marsh beyond. But Phyllis didn't seem to be listening or even looking very hard. After a glance over her shoulder at the expanse of lake behind her, she said, "Well, now, why don't we go up along the far side a little way? We don't need to row all the way around the lake, I wouldn't ask you to do that, but far enough to get the view of the lodge and the cabins and so on. . . . And then maybe we could cut across."

Wanda followed her glance. If you thought of Heron Lake as a kind of elongated clock face, where they were now at the south end would be six o'clock, with the dock at about eight. Except for a red canoe skimming around at the north end, there were only two other boats out on the lake—someone fishing close to the Potter's shore at about ten o'clock and Mrs. Rowan in her usual spot between three and four, gazing through her binoculars at the thickly wooded eastern shoreline.

Wanda took a second look at the fisherman and realized it must be Mr. Farnsworth, taking a turn at Old Rusty. Old Rusty was a legendary large brown trout that lived in that vicinity; people had been trying to catch him for years. The mystery of Phyllis's sudden enthusiasm for boating was explained.

The wind was coming up as Wanda rowed slowly along the east side of the lake, passing again the fallen tree where Andrew had found his frog. By the time Phyllis said they might as well cut across now and Wanda turned the bow away from shore to face the open water, she found she was rowing directly into a steady breeze.

"Can't you head up that way a little more, dear?" Phyllis asked after a while. She had adopted what she must have thought of as a boating pose (Wanda vaguely remembered seeing something of the kind in a picture once), leaning back against the stern and trailing her fingers in the water, her face lifted to the sky as if it were pouring sunbeams down on her instead of beginning to sprinkle with rain.

Wanda tried, but it was hard pulling, especially now they were out in the middle of the lake. Her armpits were beginning to ache; also she was starting to worry that there might be a real leak in the bottom of the boat, not just rainwater. She was relieved when Phyllis abandoned her pose in favor of making a great show of bailing as they slowly pulled closer to Mr. Farnsworth. Never mind that he wasn't even looking in their direction; if Phyllis thought bailing was going to make a better impression, that was fine with Wanda.

"Oh, Wanda," Phyllis said casually, ignoring Wanda's struggles to keep the bow steady against the wind, "would you mind going over closer to where Mr. Farnsworth is? That is Mr. Farnsworth, isn't it, in that boat with the green trim? I just remembered something I need to tell him."

"I wouldn't," Wanda said, slowing down and relaxing her grip on the oars. It felt good to rest for a moment. "He hates anyone coming near him when he's fishing."

"Well, but it'll only be for a moment," Phyllis said, straightening the brim of her hat and rearranging a windblown strand of hair so that it fell over one shoulder. "And if we get closer, I won't have to shout. Even I know better than that—it scares the fish or something."

Wanda was torn. She would have given a lot to see Phyllis's face when Mr. Farnsworth turned and snarled at her the way Wanda knew he would, maybe even yelled swear words at her. On the other hand, if there was any chance at all that Mr. Farnsworth might want to marry Phyllis, or at least take her away somewhere, Wanda didn't want to wreck it. Even considering just the short run, Phyllis had been a whole lot easier to live with since she'd started getting interested in Mr. Farnsworth. Regretfully, Wanda decided she'd better do what she could to keep them on good terms.

She shook her head and said in a deliberately whiny voice, "I'm tired of rowing." When Phyllis merely looked irritated at this, Wanda added, "And besides, I think there's a thunderstorm coming. We shouldn't be out on the water if there's going to be lightning around."

"Oh, Wanda, you're always worrying about *something*." But Phyllis glanced at the sky a bit apprehensively, aware of Wanda's reputation as a weather prophet. "I haven't heard any thunder."

"And besides that," Wanda said, playing her ace, "I think this boat may be going to sink."

Phyllis looked down at the water lapping around her ankles. "It does seem to have gotten deeper, doesn't it?" She frowned. "Oh, for heaven's sake, Wanda, why did you have to pick *this* boat, when there were all those others to choose from? Well, I suppose you'd better row us back before it gets any worse. And the rain, too," she added, as if noticing it for the first time.

She looked over at Mr. Farnsworth. He had just made another cast and was sitting hunched over, intent on his line, the brim of his slouch hat pulled down over his ears. "At least if it keeps on raining, Drew will be coming back in, too, before long."

Wanda turned the bow of the rowboat toward the dock, bending over the oars to hide a smile. This was just the kind of weather fishermen liked, she knew from watching Gus. If it didn't rain any harder than this, Mr. Farnsworth would probably stay out on the lake for the rest of the afternoon.

"You'd better keep bailing," she told Phyllis.

"I don't see how this little thing is going to do any good," Phyllis grumbled, scooping up a canful of water and flinging it over the side. "You'd think they'd give you something bigger, or a different shape anyway, more like a pitcher."

"Maybe you could use your hat," Wanda said, deadpan.

As Phyllis straightened, eyeing Wanda suspiciously, the red canoe shot by with Angie Hyatt kneeling amidships, paddling expertly. She waved and flashed a smile over her shoulder as she streaked on toward the dock. "Now if we'd taken out one of *those* instead of this big old heavy boat," Phyllis said, "we'd be back at the dock by now."

When Wanda didn't answer, Phyllis said spitefully, "But of course I suppose you'd be worried about tipping over in a canoe. I mean, never mind that you can swim, how terrible to be out in the middle of a lake without a map or a compass or any *blazes* to follow."

She sloshed some more water out of the boat. "That's a real cute kid, that Angie," she went on pointedly. "So pretty, with those eyes and that ash-blond hair—though she really ought to use a good gel on it; fine hair tends to be so flyaway. . . . Anyway, she always looks so happy and relaxed and carefree, not like some other people I could name."

"Because she's an airhead," Wanda said—not to be nasty or even to defend herself, just stating what she considered a fact.

"Well, of course we can't all have your wonderful tidy little brains," Phyllis said, in a tone of such distaste that Wanda found herself imagining her brains packed neatly together inside her head like tiny silver-gray batteries in a kit. She smiled, which made Phyllis even madder.

Chapter 7

WHEN THEY GOT BACK to the dock, Wanda made Phyllis help her turn the rowboat over and push it up on the bank a little way so that if it did have a leak, the rain wouldn't make it any worse. Crossly Phyllis retrieved her shoes and handbag and set off back to the cabin, picking her way up the path to the road like someone who'd never gone barefoot in her whole life before. Her lavender dress was all limp and draggled now, its hem splattered with mud. Wanda looked after her with satisfaction.

Then she wandered up the short side path to the rec house, a favorite place of hers in drizzly weather, with the rain pattering softly on the roof and hissing past the wide, screened windows. Angie was in there, leafing through an old pile of *National Geographics* and looking bored. When Wanda came in, she said did Wanda want to play Ping-Pong, and Wanda said sure. She felt a momentary twinge, remembering what she'd said to Phyllis about Angie, but then she saw that Phyllis was right about Angie's being pretty. If you had hair like that, Wanda thought dispassionately, and crystal-blue eyes the color of Great Harriman on a sunny morning, along with a tanned, long-legged body that never seemed to make an awkward move, probably it didn't matter much what you had inside your head.

Together they dragged the Ping-Pong table away from the wall, found a ball without dents in it, and began to play. Since neither of them was very good, they spent a lot of time chasing the ball into corners and fishing it out from under the metal folding chairs that were stacked around the room. Actually, Angie could have played quite well if she'd bothered to concentrate instead of talking all the time—she was a natural athlete, like her brother Steve. Wanda herself concentrated on keeping track of the score.

"Oh, hey, there's something I was supposed to ask you," Angie said as she rummaged around for the ball in back of the upright piano. "Yuck, somebody's old piece of gum. . . . Now, what was it again? Oh, yeah—does your grandmother play bridge?"

"Stepgrandmother," Wanda corrected her, and shrugged. "I guess so. At least, she plays gin rummy with my dad sometimes, and she's always talking about her card sense."

"Because there are these really boring people coming tomorrow," Angie said, returning to the table, "the Curtises, that know my parents. In fact it was my parents who told them about Potter's, only now they wish they hadn't, because they're afraid they'll get stuck with them—the Curtises, I mean." She picked up her paddle and slapped the ball across the net to Wanda.

"It's my serve, I think," Wanda said, catching it.

"Anyway, all they really like to do is play bridge, and my dad hates bridge; he's strictly a poker man. So my mom thought if your grandmother would play with them, that would be a help to them, and maybe to your parents, too." Angie returned Wanda's serve into the net. "Like, there's the square dance tomorrow night, only she probably wouldn't want to go, would she? Your grandmother, I mean."

"Stepgrandmother," Wanda said again. "I think it's five to four now, so I have one more serve."

"Only they'd need a fourth."

"A fourth what?" Wanda made a dive for the ball as Angie rifled her serve back.

"A fourth person, to play bridge. Well, I guess Ray likes to play when he has time, but anyway he couldn't on square-dance night."

"Do they play for money?" Wanda asked, crawling under the table after the ball.

"I don't know. I guess so, because my dad said something about his poker money that he keeps in an old tennis-ball can on his dresser, and how he wasn't going to see any of it go into Mr. Curtis's pocket. So anyway will you ask her? Your grandmother?"

This time Wanda didn't bother correcting her. "Sure. And I think maybe I know someone she could ask to be the fourth person."

"Is it my serve?" Angie whizzed one past Wanda that didn't even bounce. "Oh, hey, I'll get it, that was my fault. . . . Well, great," she said over her shoulder, moving a lamp out of a corner, "because then my parents could go to the square dance instead of having to hang around and be polite to the Curtises, and so could yours—go to the dance, I mean, and not just sit around the lodge talking to . . . what's her name again?"

"Phyllis," Wanda supplied unhappily. So other people, too, had noticed the spineless way her parents, her mother especially, kept letting themselves get trapped into being an audience for Phyllis, who hated being left to her own devices in public. Most of the adult guests had already learned to give Phyllis a wide berth, since all she wanted to talk about was herself and the fancy country club she'd belonged to in Florida and all the celebrities she'd known in her life (most of them when she was married to Wanda's grandfather, who was a TV producer).

"Unless she *wanted* to go to the square dance," Angie added doubtfully. "But my mom said she didn't look like the type."

"No," Wanda agreed with a shudder—though she wouldn't have put it past Phyllis to get herself decked out in a dirndl skirt and peasant blouse, maybe even with one of those lace-up vests, if she thought Mr. Farnsworth was going to be there. But he never went to square dances. Wanda was pretty sure he played bridge, though.

"What's the score, do you know?" Angie was bouncing the ball up and down on her paddle distractedly. Before Wanda could answer, the door banged open and Steve came in with some of the older kids, teenagers who'd been away on an overnight.

"Oh, hey, Ping-Pong, that's just what I feel like doing," one of them said. "You guys almost done?"

Wanda was about to say they weren't when Steve called to Angie, "Ray's taking a bunch of kids bowling over in Gilead. He's got room for two more in the pickup. You want to come?"

"Sure," Angie said eagerly, dropping her paddle with a clatter. "Come on, Wanda."

The ball rolled slowly to the edge of the table and dropped off. Wanda made a grab for it and missed. It skittered across the floor toward one of the teenagers, who fielded it and looked inquiringly at Wanda. She shrugged and laid her own paddle down on the table.

"I don't know how to bowl," she told Angie, who was waiting impatiently. "I guess I'll just stay here and work on my terrarium."

"In the rain?" Angie frowned. "Oh, come on, Wanda, bowling's fun!"

Wanda hesitated. She didn't want to break her rule about trying everything at Potter's at least once; on the other hand, this wasn't going to be *at* Potter's but in a neighboring town, and not even in Vermont—Gilead was across the New

Hampshire border. Finally she shook her head. "I'd be scared of getting my fingers stuck in those little holes," she said. "And what if I dropped the ball on my foot? They're real heavy, you can tell on TV."

In the doorway, Steve rolled his eyes at the ceiling. A horn tooted outside. Angie gave Wanda a baffled blue-eyed stare, then shrugged and hurried after her brother.

Two of the older kids were playing "Chopsticks" on the piano, three more were getting out the shuffleboard cues, and the Ping-Pong table was already in use again. Suddenly the big room was full of harsh, loud noise and commotion, no longer a peaceful refuge on a rainy afternoon. Wanda crossed the floor behind the shuffleboard players and went out onto the narrow screened-in side porch that overhung the lake. Sally North was lying on the old swing couch there, reading a paperback book. Wanda was surprised; she hadn't known anyone was there.

"You want to go bowling?" she said as Sally looked up. "They have room for one more, only you better hurry, the truck's leaving right now."

"I know, I heard." Sally yawned. "Actually, I sort of like bowling, but I hate riding in the back of the pickup, especially when it's raining."

"So do I. I mean, what if the tailgate came loose when you were leaning right up against it? Or a tree could fall on you if there was a lot of wind, or a branch, anyway. And if you were going by a golf course, you might get hit by a golf ball."

Sally looked at her curiously but didn't say anything. Wanda went to stand at the screen, gazing down at the raindrops dimpling the water between the water lily pads, their white and yellow blossoms folded up stiffly now, like napkins in a fancy restaurant. She always felt a little shy around Sally. She wasn't quite sure why. Sally was a year or so older, but that wasn't it. It was more the way she was so casual and relaxed all the time, like a cat that could make itself comfortable anywhere. She was sort of sleek like a cat, too, with smooth honey-colored hair and hazel-green eyes in a rounded face with a pointed chin.

She thought Sally had gone back to reading her book until she said in a thoughtful voice, "You know what your problem is, Wanda? You have too much imagination."

"I do?" Wanda turned to stare at her.

"Yes, because how could you think up all those things to worry about if you didn't?"

Wanda thought about this for a moment, then gave an uncertain nod. "I guess *you* never worry about things, do you?" she asked a bit wistfully.

Sally considered. "Well, only about important stuff, like atom bombs and earthquakes and hurricanes. Or if there was an ax murderer on the loose, hiding out in the woods somewhere, I'd worry about that. Not that anything like that would ever happen here," she added hastily at Wanda's look of alarm. "I only thought of it because of this mystery book I'm reading." She held up the paperback, which had a picture of a screaming girl in ski clothes on the cover. "You ever read mysteries?"

"No." Wanda didn't even like watching them on TV, in case the actors got hurt. Even being stabbed by a fake knife with a collapsible handle could probably give you a bad bruise, she thought, to say nothing of what could happen during car chases and falls off cliffs and escapes from burning buildings.

"Well, hey, maybe that's what you *should* do." Sally sat up with what for her was unusual energy, making the couch springs screech. "Sure, that's probably exactly what you should do, Wanda. I don't mean the kind of books that are all scary and bloody, but the ones where some detective is trying to figure out who the murderer is and who's going to get killed next. There's a whole bunch of mystery books like that up in the lodge, in that shelf on the left when you come in. You'd be good at figuring them out, I bet. And, like, then you could worry all you want about bad stuff happening, only it wouldn't be *real*, see?"

Wanda didn't think this would work somehow, but she was too gratified by Sally's interest to say so. "I might try it," she agreed.

"Who knows," Sally went on, "maybe you could even be a detective when you grow up. I mean, a person that's always looking for trouble . . . well, that's what a detective does, right?"

Wanda looked at her to see if she was teasing and decided she wasn't. "I think I'd rather be a doctor," she confided shyly. "That's sort of what they do, too."

Sally blinked; her own father was a doctor, but somehow she didn't think he'd ever thought of his work in quite this way. "Well, yeah, sort of," she said, and settled back down with her book.

It was a good afternoon for reading, Wanda thought. Maybe she'd go up to the lodge right

now and get one of those books and take it back
to the cabin. She wanted to be there anyway
when Phyllis woke up from her nap, so she could
tell her about the new people who were coming,
the ones who liked to play bridge for money.

Chapter 8

THE LEAVES OF THE WHITE BIRCH tree outside Wanda's window were green-gold with morning sunlight, quivering a little in a soft stir of air that might have been no more than the breaths of all the singing birds. Wanda woke up and stretched and wondered why she felt so happy. Then she remembered last night. It was the best time she'd ever had at a Potter's square dance, mainly because of a new kid named Hugh.

Wanda was light on her feet, with a good sense of rhythm, but of course she always worried about hearing the calls wrong or getting them mixed up—bowing to her partner when she should be bowing to her corner or going around the wrong way in do-si-do.

Last night, though, no mistake Wanda made would even have been noticed in the general confusion caused by Hugh Curtis. He'd never done square dancing before and didn't know what any of the calls meant, but that didn't keep him from joining in enthusiastically, hopping and twirling and jumping like an energetic but ill-coordinated flea. Since he was always either behind the beat while he figured out what he was supposed to be doing or ahead of it in his hurry to catch up, any square Hugh was part of immediately became a hopeless tangle. At least he didn't seem to mind people laughing at him, the way Wanda would have. Or maybe he was just such a hyper type he never even noticed.

Meanwhile, Hugh's aunt and uncle played bridge up in the lodge with Phyllis and Mr. Farnsworth. The one time Wanda peeked in on them, all four were leaning silently back in their chairs, studying a hand that had just been dealt. In the light of the bridge lamp, Wanda saw Phyllis slowly wink one large mascaraed eye at Mr. Farnsworth, who pretended not to notice. But Wanda thought the set of his shoulders expressed satisfaction. Mr. and Mrs. Curtis, by contrast, looked rather grim. Altogether Wanda considered the Curtises a timely addition to Potter's guest list.

It was still early, with Andrew just a blanket-covered lump in the bed opposite and breakfast a good hour away. Wanda heard heavy boots out on the porch steps—Pierre, coming to start the fire in the Franklin stove. She pulled the covers up under her chin and lay savoring the cool, pine-scented air, thinking what a beautiful sunny day it was going to be for the picnic at Silver Beach. The front door banged open; Pierre whistled, coughed, whistled again, and set down a stack of logs with a thump. Wanda thought how she'd even danced with Gus last night—not on purpose, of course, they'd just happened to land opposite each other during a double circle when the music stopped. Still, Gus hadn't scowled any more than usual when he'd had to put his arm around Wanda's waist and promenade her home.

Pierre coughed again. Wanda frowned. She slid out of bed, pulled on her bathrobe, and went out into the little living room, where Pierre was just touching a match to the kindling.

"Morning, missy," he said, with his broad smile that made a hundred little wrinkles in the leather of his face. Pierre never addressed anybody by name, not even guests he'd known for years. The women were "missus," the men "sir," the girls "missy," and the boys "young sir." He adjusted the dampers and got stiffly to his feet, coughing again.

"Could I get you some cough medicine, Pierre?" Wanda asked. "We have this stuff my mom always brings along for me and Andrew in case we get a cold, and it doesn't even taste too bad. Cough medicine," she repeated, as Pierre looked puzzled, and thumped herself on the chest.

"Oh—cough. No, no, not a cold, missy, just age. Many years, you understand? Lungs not so good anymore." He lifted his shoulders in a resigned little shrug and turned to go.

"Maybe you have an allergy," Wanda said. "I heard you sneezing a lot yesterday, around back in the car shed when you were fixing Mrs. Rowan's flat tire."

Pierre turned back to her politely, his face inquiring. Wanda demonstrated with a loud, "A-choo!" and his expression cleared. He nodded and laughed.

Wanda wished she knew French. She couldn't think how to explain about allergies in just a few words that Pierre would understand, especially how you weren't necessarily born with them but could start getting them anytime, maybe even when you were as old as Pierre. This was one of the things Wanda herself worried about every time she sneezed unexpectedly or had a skin irritation that might turn out to be the beginning of an allergy-type rash from eating something she liked but would never be able to eat again, like peanut butter or scrambled eggs.

Pierre waited for her to say something more, then nodded again, said cheerfully, "Well, going to be a fine, hot day, missy," and left. From the window Wanda watched him go slowly along the path to Pine Grosbeak next door, sunlight flickering down through the trees onto the back of his plaid shirt.

A door opened in the little hallway off the living room. Wanda turned guiltily as Phyllis came into the room, tying the sash of her peach satin dressing gown that clashed with her hair. This time it would be Wanda's fault for waking her up, not just Pierre's, what with their talking and her loud fake coughing and sneezing.

But to Wanda's surprise, Phyllis didn't even look mad. She yawned and said, "Oh, it's going to be a gorgeous day, isn't it? Plug the coffeepot in, would you, Wanda? Except not really good fishing weather, I guess—though why the fish should care one way or another is beyond me." She smoothed her lace-trimmed lapels and added with a secretive little smile, "Of course, it all depends on what you hope to catch."

"Fishing?" Wanda echoed, moving automatically to switch on the small coffeepot that sat on the corner of the desk blotter.

"Yes, Drew's going to take me out with him today and teach me how to fly-cast or angle or whatever it's called—isn't that sweet of him? I told him all I'd ever done was plain old fishing with worms and things, which I'm afraid was stretching the truth just a bit. I mean, I don't even like *eating* fish, as you know, except for shellfish, and as for having anything to do with a worm . . . ugh!" Phyllis paused, then crinkled her eyes in the way Wanda knew she thought was irresistible. "But you won't tell on me, I'm sure, will you, dear?"

Wanda shook her head no, she wouldn't, feeling a bit dazed. This should have been good news, but somehow she felt it wasn't. "You'll have to be really quiet, though," she said, blurting out the first thing that came into her head. "I mean, I never heard of Mr. Farnsworth taking someone fishing with him before. I guess it'll be okay if you just copy him and do what he says, but he wouldn't want anyone *talking*."

"Well, really, Wanda!" Phyllis gave an irritated little laugh. "I'm sure I'm capable of being as quiet as anyone else if the need arises. As for what Drew does and doesn't want, well"—she preened a little, toying with one of her red ringlets—"I hardly think he'd have invited me in the first place if he hadn't wanted the pleasure of my company."

All Wanda could think was that Mr. Farnsworth must have gotten carried away last night by winning a lot of money at bridge. As if to confirm this, Phyllis said dreamily as she turned toward the bathroom, "We had such a pleasant evening of cards last night . . . born partners, I think we both felt it. Oh, the Curtises play quite a nice game of bridge, I don't mean that, and naturally they're looking forward to a return match tonight, but I'm afraid they weren't really in our league once the chemistry between us began working—between Drew and me, I mean. Really, it was almost uncanny at times."

As she moved away, Wanda said urgently, "But if you go fishing, you'll miss the picnic at Silver Beach. It's really pretty there, way down at the end of Great Harriman—there's lots of sand, and the water's really warm because of the way it's so shallow. I mean, you could swim and everything, and the food's super. We all collect driftwood for the fire, and usually there's watermelon for dessert—"

But Phyllis wasn't really listening. "Oh, for heaven's sake, Wanda, I can swim any old time. And as for lunch, I'll be perfectly happy with whatever the kitchen puts up in the way of a picnic. Drew's taking care of all that, of course."

She went on into the bathroom and closed the door. Wanda stood looking helplessly after her for a moment. Then she sighed, ate one of the Fig Newtons from her windbreaker pocket, and went out on the porch to read until it was time to get dressed and go to breakfast.

She'd already finished one mystery book and was partway through another. In this one, a man had been found dead in a library—not a public library but a library right in his own house— while about a dozen people he'd invited for the weekend were doing things like playing billiards and drinking brandy and acting out charades in the living room and kissing each other in the conservatory, whatever that was.

Except one of them wasn't really doing what they said they were; one of them had gone in the library and shot Sir Malcolm and gone out again through some French windows, leaving the door locked on the inside. They'd tried to make it look like the head gardener (who had just been fired by Sir Malcolm) by wearing a pair of his boots and leaving prints in the flower bed outside, only it turned out the French windows had been bolted since shortly after dinner—Anthony Price-Clements said so. Of course he might have been lying. No one had heard the shot because of a violent thunderstorm in progress at the time.

Anyway, now it looked as if the murderer had struck again. No one had seen beautiful, spoiled Victoria Neville since breakfast, when she'd announced her intention of doing some sketching down in the old summerhouse. Lady Brenda Pomeroy said this was just an excuse to have a rendezvous with the disreputable but charming Rodney Farr, but then everyone knew Lady Brenda was jealous of Victoria. Now the detective had spotted a break in the shrubbery beyond the croquet lawn, as if something heavy might have been dragged through there. . . .

None of this was the kind of thing Wanda normally worried about in real life, except possibly for the thunderstorm. (It was true that thunder could cover up other and possibly more important loud noises, like a plane that was about to crash into your house, giving you no time to run outside.) She found it all rather peculiar, but quite enjoyable.

Chapter 9

MOST OF THE ADULTS AND LITTLE KIDS were going to Silver Beach by rowboat or canoe, with the teenagers appropriating the camp's two sailfish and the rest taking the trail that angled through the woods to the southern end of Great Harriman. Supplies for the picnic would be ferried over in the old motor launch that was stored in the boathouse next to the swimming area. Its engine wasn't very reliable, but if it conked out, someone in a rowboat could always give it a tow.

Wanda and Rita had agreed to walk over together—no big deal, since they'd be with all the other kids, too; it was more a way of showing they both still wanted to try to be friends. Rita was planning to take along her snorkeling equipment, which she'd only ever gotten to use once before, on vacation in Hawaii. When Wanda said doubtfully that she didn't think there'd be much to see underwater at Silver Beach, which was pretty but not like Hawaii, Rita said there might be eels, at least.

Wanda decided she'd pretend to be cold or getting a cramp if Rita offered to lend her the mask and snorkel. She didn't really want to know what she was swimming over, and if something happened to flicker against her ankle when she put her foot down, she'd just as soon think of it as a weed or maybe a small, friendly minnow.

As Wanda went past the lodge, she saw Nora working in the shady flower bed that sloped toward the rec house, down on her hands and knees among the begonias and coralbells with a bushel basket beside her. Wanda hesitated for a moment, then turned and went over to speak to her.

"Can't you come to the picnic, Nora?" she said shyly. "I could help you do that later, maybe, if it's only just weeding. I mean, I don't know anything about flowers, but I could help pull stuff out."

Nora sat back on her heels and gave Wanda her rare smile, which softened her rather blunt features and lit up her dark blue eyes. "Thanks, Wanda, that's really sweet of you. But no, the weeds give me a nice excuse for *not* going." When Wanda looked at her blankly, she explained, "Think how peaceful and quiet it's going to be around here for a few hours, with almost everyone off at Silver Beach."

Wanda hadn't thought of that, or in fact imagined what it must be like to run a place like Potter's when you were a quiet, private sort of person like Nora. Now, looking at it from Nora's point of view, she could understand that the beach picnic was a treat for her, too, only in a different way. She was about to turn away when something else occurred to her. "I was talking to Pierre this morning about the way he's always coughing . . . you know?"

"Yes, I'm afraid Pierre's not too well these days," Nora said, looking troubled. "I've tried to get him to see a doctor, but he keeps telling me old age is all that's wrong with him, also that weak lungs run in his family. If they do, it's news to me—his father's still alive at age ninety-six, and his mother was milking the family cow right up until the day she died, at about ninety."

Wanda explained her idea about allergies. A thought struck her. "Is Pierre doing anything different this year?" she asked. "I mean anything he didn't used to do before?"

"As a matter of fact . . ." Nora frowned down at the trowel she held in one gloved hand. "Do you know, one thing that *is* different is I've had him helping Karen out at the stables this summer, mucking out stalls and so on, and letting Hal take over some of the heavier work." Hal was the odd-job man who came over two or three times a week from the village of West Eliot near the Canadian border-crossing. "Pierre hates anything to do with horses—actually I think he's scared of them, only of course he won't admit it—and I think his feelings were a bit hurt, but I thought it would be easier on him. . . . My goodness, do you suppose that's all it is—an allergy? Just good old hay fever?"

Wanda left her pondering this and hurried around back of the lodge to catch up with Rita and the others. They'd already started off along the broad lake trail, though Wanda was pleased to see that Rita was hanging back and looking over her shoulder.

"Here," she said, as Wanda came up to her, "maybe you could carry one of my flippers. I forgot how heavy they are."

Rita was wearing her purple bathing suit with a beach towel knotted around her waist and her hiking boots, of course. Most of the other kids just had on their suits, too, some with T-shirts on over them. Wanda was the only one wearing jeans or carrying a beach bag. As usual, she also had her canteen and her red windbreaker.

"I brought some suntan lotion," she told Rita, stuffing the flipper awkwardly into the beach bag. "You can get really burned over there. There was a little kid last year that almost got sick from sunburn, and he had red hair and light skin just like you do."

Rita looked offended. "My hair's strawberry-blond, not red, and anyway I never burn. But thanks, anyway," she said gruffly, as Wanda's face fell.

Up ahead, Steve turned with a laugh. "Come on, guys, we've got to find *something* for Wanda to worry about today. I mean, it's not going to rain, and there's hardly any wind, so she can't worry about giant waves or sailboats tipping over and people getting drowned. And if we meet a moose or a grizzly bear on the trail, Rita can always shoot 'em with her trusty spear gun."

Wanda looked in alarm at the object hanging from Rita's wrist, then saw it was only her snorkel. Everyone laughed at her expression. It was good-natured laughter, though, and although the teasing stung a little, Wanda found she didn't mind it too much.

Of course she wasn't going to tell anybody she already had a worry, the one about Phyllis and Mr. Farnsworth. She'd glimpsed them setting off about an hour ago, also heading for the lake trail. Usually if Mr. Farnsworth wasn't fishing on Heron Lake, he went over to Little Harriman or up to one of the Canadian lakes. Motorboats were allowed on Great Harriman—sometimes there were even water-skiers, people from the summer houses and cottages scattered around its miles of shoreline—and so it was avoided by most of the serious fishermen.

Today, though, Mr. Farnsworth must have decided Great Harriman was good enough for taking Phyllis fishing and would also allow plenty of room for any wild casts she made. He might also have thought she'd be less noticeable there. He was wearing his usual dun-colored fishing clothes and slouch hat, whereas Phyllis had on her own idea of fishing garb—a kind of loose-fitting turquoise pajama suit printed with large white and orange flowers. With it she wore the large sun hat with the veil that tied under her chin—a different veil this time, turquoise to match her outfit. Wanda thought if the bright weather didn't keep the fish away from the surface of the water, Phyllis's reflection certainly would.

The narrow trail to Silver Beach slanted off from the main lake trail well before the picnic and swimming area, so Wanda had no view of the water until finally the trees thinned and the trail joined the shoreline as it curved around toward the deltalike expanse of fine, silky sand at the lake's southern end. A driftwood fire had already been started in the center of the broad beach, its flames pale in the brilliant light. Down at the water's edge, Terence the cook, wearing only cutoffs and his tall chef's hat, was waving his long arms about as he supervised the helpers wading ashore from the launch with boxes of food and supplies.

From here, though, you couldn't see the main part of the big lake, where Phyllis and Mr. Farnsworth would be. Wanda kept trying, but there were too many wooded curves and bulges of land in the way. They'd probably be much too far up the lake to distinguish from here, anyway.

"Why do you keep looking over your shoulder?" Rita demanded suspiciously from behind her; she was on the alert for anything Wanda might start worrying about. Then she laughed. "Oh, look, here comes that new kid, that Hugh."

He was floundering along the trail behind them, encumbered by a large rubber raft that kept catching on vines and bushes. "Hey, you guys, wait up!" he called. Rita giggled as he caught one of his flip-flops on a root, tripped, and went sprawling. All the kids knew better than to wear flip-flops on the trail. But Hugh's expression as he picked himself up again was as eager as ever, his eyes shining under his overgrown brown crewcut that stuck straight up in the air, seeming to pull his eyebrows with it. "Are we almost there?" he asked.

Wanda realized guiltily that probably no one had thought to look for Hugh or even check whether he was going on the picnic. His aunt and uncle were staid, sedentary types who were probably having their lunch in the dining room, attended today by Doris as both cook and waitress. Wanda frowned at Rita to stop laughing at him. Then she saw that Hugh had a pair of binoculars slung around his skinny neck, and stopped short, letting Rita go on by. "Hey, can I borrow those?" she said, pointing.

"Sure," he said, and wrenched them off so hastily he almost took his head off with them. "Oh, wow, is that the beach? It looks super."

Wanda nodded absently. She'd spotted a small, sandy, grass-tufted point of land sticking out into the water just ahead. Walking cautiously to the edge, she trained the binoculars on the long northward sweep of the lake. The lenses were so powerful she almost jumped away from a red speedboat that seemed to be heading straight at her.

After a few moments, though, she found what she was looking for—a rowboat anchored offshore well beyond the Potter's swimming area, where the land bulged out again, not far from the place where she and Gus and Steve had caught the frogs. There were two figures in the boat, and though she couldn't make them out clearly, she could see the wide brim of Phyllis's hat.

Phyllis didn't seem to be fishing. Maybe she was unpacking the lunch and complaining about the stodgy white bread (never mind that it was homemade) and too much mayonnaise. Wanda felt relieved. She didn't know quite what she'd expected to see, but the scene looked peaceful and companionable enough.

At the thought of lunch, her stomach growled. "Here," she said, and thrust the binoculars at Hugh, who was hovering behind her, trying to see over her shoulder. Clutching her beach bag, she ran to catch up with the others.

Chapter 10

TRANSPORT WAS MORE OR LESS REVERSED on the way back from Silver Beach, with most of the kids going back by boat and the adults saying they'd had enough sun for one day and needed to walk off their lunches, anyway. Wanda found herself in the last boat to leave the beach, a big four-seater, with Mrs. Rowan at the oars. With her were Angie, Gus, Sally, several large plastic bags of nonburnable trash, and a cranky little kid named Justin, who'd balked at going back along the trail, even after his father offered to carry him. At the last minute he'd been dumped unceremoniously onto the middle seat between Angie and Gus, who dried his tears and managed to buckle a small-sized life vest on him before he fell asleep with his head against Angie's shoulder.

Gus had offered to row, but Mrs. Rowan had said no, she hated having anyone else row when she was in a boat; she was just the same way about cars and driving. She said this casually, with a laugh, as she pulled away from the shore with a long, steady stroke, but Wanda thought she was mainly sparing Gus's feelings. Although he was wiry and strong for his age, Gus wasn't very big; Wanda could see it might have been a long trip back with Gus at the oars, considering their heavy load.

In fact, the boat was riding quite low in the water, Wanda noticed a bit nervously from her perch in the bow. Maybe Wanda, since she was lighter, should change places with Sally, who was in the stern with the trash bags, or at least have Sally pass one of the bags up front. Or maybe it was the middle seat that needed lightening. If Wanda sat in the middle seat with Gus, and Angie moved up front, and Sally stayed where she was but got rid of one of the bags and took Justin back in the stern with her—

"So good of all you kids to help with the cleanup," Mrs. Rowan said, erasing this complicated diagram by turning to include Wanda in her pleasant smile. "I wish I could say the same for my granddaughter, but it appears she's had too much sun. I did tell her to wear a hat, but"—she shrugged—"who listens to advice from an old-fogy grandmother?"

Rita had left with the first group to return along the trail, saying she had a headache. Her face was shiny-red, and so were her shoulders and the back of her neck from all the time she'd spent floating in the water with her snorkel, looking mostly at the stubs of drowned trees and an occasional small crayfish.

"I told her, too," Wanda said. "About watching out for the sun, I mean." Somehow this sounded rude, as if she'd agreed with Mrs. Rowan about her being an old fogy, which wasn't what she thought at all, so she added quickly, "I'm sure she would have helped if she'd still been there."

She didn't feel it necessary to explain that her own main reason for always being one of the last to leave a cookout was to make sure the fire was really out. When no one was looking, Wanda always got a last cupful of water—or used her canteen—and dribbled it carefully over the ashes.

"Oh, wow," Angie said, then lowered her voice hastily as Justin stirred and took his thumb out of his mouth. "You mean Rita has *sunstroke*?"

"No, no—just what people used to call a touch

of the sun," Mrs. Rowan reassured her. "Nothing a couple of aspirin won't cure, and some time spent lying down in a dark room."

Sally yawned, lounging into a more comfortable position on the stern seat. "Sounds good to me," she said, and added contentedly, "It was a neat picnic, though."

"Wasn't it? I thought Terence really outdid himself with those angel food cupcakes for Nan Kirby's birthday. And then your father winning the three-legged race with that funny little Curtis boy—" Mrs. Rowan broke off suddenly to say, "Look, everyone, a loon!"

They all looked where she was pointing but couldn't see anything except a blank expanse of water glittering in the afternoon light.

"It just dived," Mrs. Rowan explained. She'd stopped rowing in order to consult her wristwatch. "Fourteen, fifteen . . . They often stay down for as long as two minutes, you know, and that's just an ordinary dive—I believe they're capable of submerging for ten and even fifteen minutes at a time. . . . Twenty-one, twenty-two . . ."

Wanda stared obediently into the dazzle, hoping they wouldn't encounter too many more diving loons on the way back to camp; otherwise it might be an even longer trip than if Gus had taken the oars. It was very quiet now that Mrs. Rowan had stopped rowing, the only sounds the soft lapping of the water against the sides of the boat and the distant mosquito-whine of a speed-boat at the far end of the lake.

"There he is!" Mrs. Rowan checked her watch again as a sleek head broke the surface, followed by the bulky, speckle-feathered body of the big bird. "Two minutes, fourteen seconds. My, that really was a dive!"

Gus said, "What's the record, do you know? For a bird diving, I mean?"

Mrs. Rowan was one of the few adults Gus ever spoke to at Potter's besides Pierre. They started talking about grebes and sea ducks and penguins, but Wanda was no longer listening. As Mrs. Rowan took up the oars again, she sat twisted around in her seat, squinting along the shoreline past the Potter's swimming area, which was just coming into view now—the raft offshore, the broad flat rocks and narrow slice of beach, the picnic tables in the grassy clearing behind.

"Mrs. Rowan," she interrupted, "could I use your glasses? Your binoculars?"

"Why, you could, Wanda, certainly, if I had them with me, but for once I don't. I hate getting sand in them, and anyway there's not much good birding down around Silver Beach at this time of year. . . . Why?" She turned her head inquiringly.

"It's just . . . well, can you see how many people are in that boat?" Wanda pointed. "The one way up by that bend, see? Where there's a big sort of shaggy-looking bush hanging out over the water?"

Mrs. Rowan slowed her stroke to gaze over her shoulder. "Only one person, I think. But then I'm a bit nearsighted."

"Yeah, just somebody out fishing," Gus said, shading his eyes to look where Wanda was pointing. "That's a place I sometimes try, too, for bass."

Wanda frowned. Where was Phyllis, then? Because the lone fisherman certainly wasn't Phyllis, who didn't even know how to row a boat.

"Should there be someone else, dear?" Mrs. Rowan asked, a puzzled look on her handsome, weatherbeaten face.

Wanda hesitated. She didn't want to have to explain about Phyllis and Mr. Farnsworth; it would be too embarrassing. "I just happened to notice there were two people before," she said lamely. "When we were going to Silver Beach, I mean. So I just wondered."

"Oh, hey!" Sally roused herself from her sprawl in the stern. "The mystery of the missing fisherman!" she exclaimed gleefully. "Right, Wanda?"

"Oh, what's Wanda worrying about now?" Angie said fretfully, shifting under Justin's weight. "Gosh, this is a heavy kid, and so *sandy*."

"Maybe one of them conked the other over the head with an oar," Sally went on, "and then pushed him over the side. Except I guess he'd have to weigh him down first, like with rocks in his pockets or something. I mean, you wouldn't want the body to float and give the whole deal away."

Wanda winced. This was coming too close for comfort to her own worst worry about Phyllis and Mr. Farnsworth. Putting it into words should have made it sound dumb, but somehow it didn't.

"More likely one of them just wanted to go ashore and the other rowed him in and let him off," Mrs. Rowan said practically, turning the bow of their own boat toward shore.

"Yeah, except there's no good place to land up that way," Gus said. "The nearest place is down by our beach."

They were heading in toward the boathouse now, set back in a natural cleft between the big sloping rocks where the rowboats were kept beached. Wanda looked at the rocks farther along to see if maybe Phyllis was sunning herself there. But probably she would have had enough sun by now. If she'd gotten tired of fishing, or wasn't feeling well or something, and Mr. Farnsworth had rowed her back in as Gus said, she would have walked back over the trail to camp. By now, Wanda told herself, Phyllis was probably asleep in her room back at Kingfisher, stretched out flat on her bed with her white mask over her eyes.

Wanda told herself all this; she also told herself it was a good thing Mr. Farnsworth was too far away for anyone to have recognized him, because then they'd be sure to guess that the person Wanda was worrying about was her own horrible stepgrandmother.

But maybe that was wrong of her. Maybe she should tell Mrs. Rowan she was worried something might have happened to Phyllis, never mind how the kids would laugh at her, and ask her to row on up the shore until they got within calling distance of the other boat. Mrs. Rowan wouldn't be afraid of calling to Mr. Farnsworth

when he was fishing, and she was pretty sure
Mr. Farnsworth wouldn't dare yell at her and
shake his fist and order her to go away again.
Unless, of course, he had something to hide.

Chapter 11

BUT IT WAS TOO LATE. Mrs. Rowan had already shipped her oars, and they were gliding in over shelving rock flecked gold with mica and bits of gravel in the clear, sunlit water. There was nothing for Wanda to do but jump out and grab the painter as the bow bumped gently against the granite slope, then help hold the boat steady while everyone got out. They unloaded it and dragged it up onto dry rock well above the waterline while Mrs. Rowan put the oars away in the boathouse. Justin woke up even crankier than he'd been before. He refused to be carried, but he wouldn't walk, either. Angie and Gus had to make a chair seat of their hands just to get him across the picnic area to the start of the trail. Once there, he revived suddenly and scooted off like a beetle released from under a jar, shrieking happily as he ran.

Wanda helped Sally stuff the trash bags into the big cans at the edge of the picnic ground. Then she lingered by one of the tables, taking her time about getting her windbreaker out of her beach bag to wear back through the woods, also her canteen, which was easier to carry slung around her neck, especially since she now had both of Rita's swim flippers in the bag.

"Coming, Wanda?" Mrs. Rowan had paused with Sally at the entrance to the trail, which arched away beyond them invitingly like a wide, leafy tunnel.

"In a minute," Wanda called back.

Their voices faded. Wanda stood irresolute, looking around at the peaceful setting in its dappling of afternoon sunlight. Leaving the bag on the table, she went down onto the little beach. Because of the way the land curved, she couldn't see Mr. Farnsworth's boat from here, not even when she picked her way out over the tumble of small rocks that formed a rough breakwater at the far end of the beach.

"Phyllis?" she called.

A Canada jay scolded from the trees behind her, and a mother duck gave her a beady-eyed glance as she led her little flotilla of ducklings in a straight line from the corner of the raft to a clump of reeds beyond where Wanda stood.

Wanda sighed. She retraced her steps, took off her windbreaker and tied it around her waist, reslung her canteen around her neck, and set off along the shore trail. She knew from experience that when a worry started nagging at her this way, there was nothing to do except check it out. It seemed unfair that the worry had to be about Phyllis, a person she detested; but since there was no one else around to worry about her, Wanda supposed she was stuck with it.

After a few minutes the trail gave her a distant view of the rowboat through a gauzy screen of trees and bushes. Mr. Farnsworth's back was to her, but he looked the way he always did when he was fishing—sitting hunched and still, intent on his line, his hat pulled down around his ears. Wanda wasn't sure, but she thought the boat was farther out in the lake than it had been that morning, as if he'd rowed a little distance and reanchored. You couldn't go very far from shore and still anchor, because the lake was so deep.

She lost sight of him as she trudged on, then saw him again, closer and clearer as the trail hugged the outward curve of the shore. He'd reeled in his line and was making a new cast—

a powerful motion of his arm and wrist that sent the line snaking out over the water to land with barely a ripple on the smooth surface. As Wanda stood watching, he lowered himself onto the seat, the boat rocked gently, and all was as still and motionless again as if she were looking at a painted picture of a man fishing.

Mr. Farnsworth certainly didn't look as if he had anything more on his mind than catching a bass, Wanda told herself. She also told herself that she was within shouting distance now. Only what was she going to say? It would sound pretty funny to yell, "What have you done with Phyllis?" Also it wasn't what you would call a subtle approach. In the mysteries she'd been reading, the detective always did a lot of sleuthing and snooping around before he came right out in the open and yelled at people.

On the other hand, Wanda thought, this wasn't exactly a complicated situation like the ones in the books. Phyllis had been in the boat with Mr. Farnsworth, and now she wasn't. Unless . . . could she still be in the boat, only down on the bottom, lying there out of sight? *Pushed* there out of sight?

Wanda wished Sally had never started her reading those dumb books. Not only was she having the scariest worry she'd ever had in her whole life; it was a worry she didn't really believe in, which made it worse somehow—as if her mind had thrown out a wild cast that would surely scare away any sensible fish in the vicinity. She shook her head at herself and started forward again, deciding she'd at least get to where Mr. Farnsworth could see her before she yelled at him.

Then something to the right of the trail ahead caught her eye—one of her own yellow blazes, on a sapling a few yards up the bank. This was exactly where they'd caught the frogs that day, Wanda realized, down in that muddy little cove with the big rock just offshore. . . .

Wanda stopped dead, looking at the mud. In it was a clear footprint with a waffle design, like the one on the soles of Phyllis's wedge-heeled canvas shoes. Not only that, there was another, fainter print of the same design on the trail just ahead of her, crossing it. She looked again at the sapling she'd marked and saw that the damp leaves on the bank looked freshly scuffed and turned over, as if someone had climbed up there recently.

With a last puzzled stare at the motionless fisherman and his rod, Wanda left the trail and scrambled up the slope, her canteen banging against her thigh. It was only about ten yards or so to the narrow side trail they'd come down that day, marked by another yellow Magic Marker blob on a birch tree at the edge.

Wanda hesitated. Which way would Phyllis have gone? It was hard to imagine her voluntarily climbing uphill, but the downhill way to the left would just have brought her back to the shore, farther along from where Mr. Farnsworth was fishing. It was the wrong direction for heading back to camp, and besides, would Phyllis have gone that way if she was trying to get away from him? Wanda studied the trail for several yards in each direction, but it hadn't rained in several days now and the ground here was too hard to show a footprint.

"Phyllis?" Her voice sounded quavery to her own ears in the silent woods where nothing stirred, not even the motes of sunlight sifting down through the trees. But somehow she didn't want to call any louder, in case Mr. Farnsworth heard.

It was hotter up here, away from the water. Wanda redid the knot of her windbreaker around her sweaty waist, wishing her bathing suit hadn't dried from swimming, also that she'd done a better job of brushing off the sand before she put on her jeans, which felt stiff and itchy against her legs. Then she turned to the right and started climbing uphill. The trail was even steeper than she remembered, and not all that easy to follow, coming up from below. Wanda hadn't made any blazes here because of being with the boys, and, anyway, she remembered, she'd just been using her washable marker then.

Sure enough, after a few minutes she came to a place where the trail seemed to vanish altogether in a tangle of brush and fallen limbs. Turning, she could see a single faded red blaze on a tree behind her, but there was none up ahead that she could see. Well, it couldn't be all that far now up to the main Ledge trail; it was just a matter of continuing uphill. But would Phyllis have known that?

If this were happening in a book, Wanda thought tiredly, standing up on a log to see better, there'd be a scrap of material caught on a branch just about now, to go along with the footprints. Of course usually the scrap was so tiny the detective had to use his magnifying glass to make anything out of it. A magnifying glass was one thing Wanda had never thought to carry in her windbreaker pockets, though she did have an old glasses lens of her father's—useful for signaling and maybe even for starting a fire if she ran out of matches. That sounded kind of tricky, though. You had to figure out just the right angle for catching the sun's rays and then redirect them onto a little pile of dry leaves or twigs you'd collected. . . .

Wanda had been staring vaguely into a patchwork pattern of light and shade off to her right beyond a dark little grove of cedar trees. Now she realized the lower part of the patchwork included a splash of turquoise—not a color you saw much of in the woods at this or any other time of year.

She edged her way around one of the prickly cedars, then froze. Phyllis was lying on her back in the rough grass of a little clearing, in much the same position Wanda had imagined her taking her nap—stretched out full length with her arms at her sides and a pillow under her neck, her chin pointing at the ceiling. Only here of course it was sky instead of ceiling, and the pillow was her folded jacket. Instead of a sleep mask, she had her hat over her face. She'd taken off her shoes, too, and set them neatly side by side on a small flat rock next to her.

Wanda crept closer. "Phyllis?" she said.

Phyllis didn't stir. Wanda saw now that her flowery slacks were all dirty and torn, with a big rip across one knee. Under her jacket she'd been wearing a sleeveless white top, and her bare, damp-looking arms—Wanda always hated looking at Phyllis's arms—were covered with scratches and fresh insect bites beginning to swell pink like big soft pimples.

A fly settled on the back of Phyllis's hand and made its way along one of the raised veins she was always smearing some special cream on. Phyllis didn't even twitch. It occurred to Wanda, with a little lurch in the pit of her stomach, that Phyllis might not just be asleep. After all, this was a pretty strange place to lie down and take a nap, and . . . Was she even breathing?

Wanda squatted down beside her, but in the checkered light it was hard to tell for sure. If Phyllis had been hurt or feeling sick, it seemed unlikely that she would have bothered to fold up her jacket, take off her shoes, and arrange her hat over her face just so before she lay down to die. Of course, with Phyllis you never knew.

Wanda looked at the hat. She wasn't sure if she'd know if Phyllis was dead or not just by looking at her face, unless her eyes were rolled back up in her head or something equally gross.

If she had a mirror, she could hold it up to Phyllis's mouth and see if it clouded over; but a mirror was another thing Wanda had never thought to include in her windbreaker pockets.

Gingerly, like someone playing pick-up-sticks, Wanda pinched the brim of the hat between the thumb and forefinger of each hand and lifted it off Phyllis's face.

Then she sank back on her heels in relief, if only at knowing she wasn't going to have to deal with a dead body in the woods after all. Phyllis looked terrible, but she wasn't dead. Wanda could see the breath quivering in and out of her nostrils, and even hear its faint whistling sound. Mostly she looked exhausted, her skin heavy and slack where it sagged away from her jaw. Her dyed hair was all dusty and tangled, her lipstick was gone, and her mascara was smeared and gummy under eyelids that looked sore and swollen, as if she'd been crying. In fact, she looked like someone who'd cried herself to sleep.

Mixed with distaste, Wanda felt an unfamiliar stirring of something that might have been pity. For a moment, she almost felt sorry for Phyllis.

Chapter 12

THIS FEELING VANISHED IN THE NEXT MOMENT, never to return. Phyllis opened her eyes, gave a little shriek, and said, "Oh, for heaven's sake, Wanda! Why are you always creeping *up* on people?" She pressed a hand to her heart and lay still for a moment, her eyelids fluttering. Then she opened them again, eyed Wanda narrowly, and said, "What are you doing here, anyway? I thought you were off on that picnic with all the other jolly campers. If you've been hanging around spying on us—"

"I got worried when you weren't still in the boat with Mr. Farnsworth," Wanda interrupted, ignoring this. She shrugged. "So then I thought I'd better make sure you were okay."

"Well, I am not okay," Phyllis said crossly.

"Why else would I be lying here in the middle of these filthy woods? I simply couldn't go any farther. I was actually *crawling* along on my hands and knees, and then I . . . well, never mind about that. Among other things, I think I've broken my ankle." She struggled to sit up, winced, and flopped back down again. "Sprained it, anyway."

Wanda followed her glance. The ankle did look sort of puffy, the skin stretched tight and shiny. "Want me to try and get your shoe back on?"

"No. Yes." But Phyllis groaned as soon as Wanda attempted it.

"Oh, wonderful," she said between her teeth. "It's going to take a stretcher to get me out of here, probably. You'd better go back to camp and get help, Wanda. Assuming you even know where we are. I tried to follow those dumb yellow marks of yours, but a lot of help they were—they just petered out in the middle of nowhere. So then I took this little trail that went straight up, practically, and then I couldn't see it anymore, and the next thing I knew I stepped in a hole that was all piled up with leaves like an elephant trap, and my ankle turned right over—"

Wanda was only half listening, pondering the

situation. "The best way to get you back would be by boat," she said, thinking aloud. "Then someone could bring the pickup truck over on the lake trail. Except we're pretty high up from the lake now. Maybe you could sort of slide down on your bottom, and then if Mr. Farnsworth's still there—"

"Don't mention that name to me!" Phyllis snapped. "I would die before I asked Drew Farnsworth for help of any kind. The man is a maniac."

Wanda's heart sank, though she'd been expecting something of the kind. "What did he do?" she asked resignedly.

"What did he *do*? What does it look like he did? Dumped me out of his boat, that's what—just rowed over to this rock where there wasn't even anyplace to land and told me to get out. In water up to my knees, and that revolting mud underneath, I almost lost my shoes.... And then he rowed away again, leaving me to fend for myself in this wilderness. All because I wouldn't kill a fish!"

"Kill a fish?"

"Oh, it was horrible." Phyllis shuddered. "He caught this awful, slimy fish that got off the hook somehow and started flapping around in the bottom of the boat, coming straight at me and looking at me, too, I swear it did, with this big, starey eye. . . . And then when I started screaming, he told me to hit it on the head with an oar. Hit it on the head! I'd have liked to hit *him* on the head. So then I sort of grabbed for him and we both lost our balance and the boat tipped way over and his fishing box, or whatever you call it, slid off the seat, with all his precious flies in it. Never mind that I hit my knee on the oarlock and lost one of my contact lenses. And the language! Never in my life have I been spoken to that way, and not just spoken to, *yelled* at. . . ." She raised her head. "What are you doing?"

Wanda had taken an ace bandage from one of her windbreaker pockets and was starting to unroll it. "I always bring this up to Potter's out of our medicine cabinet," she explained, setting aside the safety pin she kept fastened to the end in case the Velcro seal didn't work. "You could use it for a tourniquet, too, if you happened to cut an artery or something. Let's see—I think I remember how to do this from when Mrs. Hardy next door sprained her ankle after the ice storm. You sort of crisscross it around, like this and this. . . ."

She snugged down the Velcro and fastened the

pin, too, for good measure. "Does that feel any better?"

Phyllis flexed her foot gingerly. "As a matter of fact, it does," she said grudgingly. "I might even try standing on it, if you'll help me up. Put my other shoe on first, though, will you?"

It was a struggle, but after a lot of pulling and bracing and heaving, Wanda managed to get Phyllis on her feet. Leaving her propped against a tree, Wanda hunted around until she found a long stick that was strong enough for Phyllis to use as a cane. Then she made Phyllis take a drink of water from her canteen. Phyllis said it tasted like water someone had washed their socks in, but she took several long, thirsty gulps. Next Wanda produced a tube of first-aid cream from her windbreaker and dabbed it over Phyllis's scratches and insect bites.

"I have Band-Aids, too, if you want," she offered.

"No, no, I'll just put my jacket back on, if you'll hand it to me—and my hat, too. Oh, Lord, my hair!" She raked her fingers through it, dislodging a number of twigs and leaf fragments, which she looked at with distaste. "I don't suppose you have a comb, do you?" Wanda shook her head. Phyllis sighed. "It got so hot in that boat, I just had to take my jacket off—and then Drew wouldn't let me put on any insect repellent, so of course I got eaten alive. He said the fish could smell it. I mean, I ask you!"

"Would you care for a Fig Newton?" Wanda asked, helping her on with her rumpled jacket.

"No, thank you." Phyllis laughed a little hysterically. "You know, you really are an amazing kid, Wanda. Weird but amazing. —Where are you going?" she added nervously, as Wanda crossed the clearing and stood peering through the trees on the far side.

"I just want to see how far we are from the main Ledge trail. If it isn't too far, that would be the quickest way to go back—a lot quicker than going down to the shore trail and all the way around."

"Well, I'm certainly not going anywhere near the shore if that man's still there," Phyllis told her, cramming her hat on her head and tying the veil under her chin with a savage jerk. "I wouldn't give him the satisfaction of seeing me in this condition."

Wanda thought it possible that Mr. Farnsworth had forgotten all about Phyllis for the time being, but she decided not to say so in case there was any chance of their patching things up again. In Phyllis's present mood, this didn't seem likely.

"The main trail's just on the other side of those big boulders," she reported, returning to where Phyllis stood balancing on her stick. "We can cut across through there, if you don't mind going through a sort of thicket."

"Oh, what's another thicket, more or less?" Phyllis laughed bitterly, looking down at her ruined slacks.

With Phyllis leaning heavily on Wanda's shoulder, they struggled up the slope to the comparatively level, hard-packed earth of the main trail. While Phyllis rested against a granite outcropping, Wanda tried to see if she could fit the other wedge-heeled shoe back on over the ace bandage.

"Oh, never mind," Phyllis said after a moment.

Wanda looked up at her uneasily. Her face was pale and sweaty, and she was biting her lip. If Phyllis fainted on the trail or had to throw up or something, Wanda didn't think she was capable of getting her on her feet a second time. "You probably ought to take an aspirin," she said worriedly. "Usually I have some in my pocket, but I guess I used it all up on my terrarium. It's supposed to keep the plants fresher or something."

"I have some Tylenol in my bag," Phyllis said, and scowled. "But of course my bag is still in that horrible boat. And my dark glasses, too. I suppose he'll just throw them overboard. Designer glasses, too—I paid a month's rent for them. Or it would have been a month's rent if I could afford to rent anything in the first place."

Wanda didn't attempt to make sense of this remark, beyond hoping that Phyllis wasn't going to start talking about how poor she was. If she did, Wanda would be tempted to repeat her father's words about selling some of her fancy jewelry and getting a job like any normal, healthy, self-respecting human being. To change the subject, she asked as they set off slowly along the trail, "Did you learn how to fish, at least?"

Phyllis snorted. "Every time I tried casting, I wrapped the line around my neck or snagged it on something. At least he had sense enough to leave the hook off, otherwise I'd probably be blind in both eyes by now instead of just one."

Wanda thought of offering Phyllis the lens from her father's glasses. Maybe she could stick it in her eye like a monocle. The thought made her grin. Luckily Phyllis didn't notice. She was still brooding as she limped along. Wanda saw that her pace was improving, as if maybe the exercise was helping her ankle instead of hurting it.

"And then it turned out he hadn't planned to stay anchored. No, he was expecting me to take him trawling or trolling or whatever the word is, meaning I was supposed to row him around ever so slowly while he fished. He said he thought everyone knew how to row a boat. As if it were something you were born knowing, like breathing." Phyllis stabbed angrily at the trail with her stick.

The evergreens began to thin around them, giving way to the lighter foliage of birches and hickories and maples. As the trail started to slope down toward camp, Wanda said, "I could go get help now, if you want. The last part is kind of steep."

"No, no, I can manage. As a matter of fact, Wanda . . ." Phyllis paused and then said carefully, in her most appealing tone, "I'd just as soon you didn't say anything about all this to anyone. About Drew and the boat and so on, I mean. We'll just say I was out taking a walk and I tripped on a root or something and hurt my ankle. And then you just happened to be taking a walk, too, and heard me calling for help. That's all right with you, dear, isn't it?"

Wanda nodded absently; she'd been expecting this. She was wondering how Ray and Pierre or whoever would have managed, anyway, supposing Phyllis really had needed help getting down from the Ledge. She'd be pretty heavy to carry. But maybe they could have made a chair seat out of their hands.

This picture made her smile. Phyllis saw the smile this time and said suspiciously, "Unless of course you've already blabbed to everyone about how *worried* you were. Oh, heavens, why didn't I think of that before?" She groaned. "I suppose the story's probably all over camp by now."

"No, it isn't," Wanda told her. "I mean, I didn't say anything."

"Are you sure?" Phyllis eyed her mistrustfully.

Wanda nodded again. "It would have been too embarrassing," she explained simply.

Phyllis frowned at this but then had to give all her attention to the trail as it dipped down into a sunlit hollow filled with wild asters and ferns and orange touch-me-not. The juice of the latter was supposed to be good for poison ivy, Wanda remembered; maybe she should get

Phyllis to rub some on her insect bites. But it seemed too much trouble to stop now, and besides, Phyllis would undoubtedly recoil at the idea of smearing herself with a lot of sticky plant juice.

Would Mrs. Rowan put two and two together? Wanda thought she probably would, but also that she wouldn't be interested enough to say anything. Mrs. Rowan wasn't a snob, exactly, but she didn't mix much with the other guests unless they were people she'd known for a long time. Wanda had seen her studying Phyllis once with an air of bemusement, as if Phyllis were a large exotic bird that had alighted unexpectedly among the familiar jays and nuthatches and sparrows—a parrot, say, or a macaw, some species outside her ken or range of interest.

The roof of the car shed was visible now through the trees. Wanda's steps were almost as heavy as Phyllis's as they came down the last steep stretch of trail onto the level ground by the staff dormitory. Here, by tacit agreement, they turned into the kitchen yard, crossing behind the lodge in order to avoid any watchers on the veranda in front.

Never mind that Phyllis hadn't uttered a single word of thanks, Wanda thought despondently, or that the Munsons were probably stuck with her forever, now that Mr. Farnsworth wouldn't be marrying her. No, the really depressing thing was the realization that had just occurred to her: that she, Wanda, had somehow blown her big chance to show people that sometimes the things she worried about really did happen.

Chapter 13

"WHERE'S PHYLLIS?"

Andrew came galloping up the porch steps, looking all excited about something.

"Asleep," Wanda told him. She was pressing ground pine into her terrarium while her mother sat in one of the rockers doing her needlepoint. It was about half an hour before dinner, with the tree shadows falling long across the slope and Heron Lake a quiet mirror below in the calm, late light, its far rim sheeted with silver.

"Yes, and please don't wake her, Andrew," Mrs. Munson said. "I fixed an ice pack for her ankle to ease the pain, poor thing, and she only drifted off a little while ago."

"But didn't she hear about Mr. Farnsworth?"

"She won't want to," Wanda said before she thought.

"What about him, dear?" Her mother gave her a sharp look. Even she couldn't pretend the fishing expedition had been a great success, not after the way Phyllis had come hobbling in with her clothes in tatters and her face all spotty with mosquito bites as if she had chicken pox. She'd gone straight to her room, muttering something about taking an antihistamine.

"He caught Old Rusty!" Andrew said. "He didn't keep him, he threw him back, but it was! He told what he looked like, all brown and ugly and really gigantic, and they all said it was—Ray and Pierre and everybody."

While her mother was figuring out that Old Rusty must be a fish, Wanda said, "You mean Mr. Farnsworth was out fishing on Heron Lake just now? After fishing over on Great Harriman all day?" She thought of Gus and decided she never would understand fishermen.

Andrew nodded solemnly. "He was going back to his cabin, and then he said he just had a *feeling*. So he decided to take a boat out and just make a few, you know"—he swung his arm around his head.

"Casts," Wanda supplied.

"Yeah, and on the very first one he felt this bite, and then *zoom*. Like he could tell it was a really big fish, the way it took off on him." Again Andrew demonstrated, almost knocking Wanda's terrarium off the porch railing.

"Shh!" said Mrs. Munson, glancing at Phyllis's window, which was at the corner of the cabin, beyond the porch.

"And Mr. Farnsworth was smiling," Andrew said, as if announcing that the sun had risen in the west. "He's gonna take a bunch of us kids up to Marie's for a soda after dinner, the ones that were around. I can go, can't I, Mom? It won't be really late. Oh, yeah, and that's what I was supposed to tell Phyllis—about playing bridge a half hour later than they were going to. With those new people, the Curtises."

"Oh, I doubt if Phyllis will be feeling up to bridge tonight," his mother said. "I suppose she could always put her foot up on a chair or something, but—"

"She won't want to," Wanda said again. "Play bridge, I mean."

"But she has to!" Andrew stared at her, round-eyed. "Mr. Farnsworth says she brings him luck! He says that's why he caught Old Rusty—because he had to use this old trout fly that was stuck in his hat, on account of Phyllis making him lose his tackle box."

"Oh, dear," said Mrs. Munson.

"I don't know how she did that," Andrew said, looking a little confused, "but that's what he said. Anyway, that's why he just used an old beat-up fly from his hat that he'd practically forgotten about and never even thought of trying on Old Rusty. He had to fix it with some dental floss he found in Phyllis's purse, the green kind that tastes like mint, you know? And he thinks that might have been part of it, like maybe the mint got Old Rusty's attention."

He beamed at his mother, who looked back at him blankly. "Oh, hey, that's what I forgot," he said, his expression changing. "I was supposed to bring Phyllis's purse and stuff back to her, but I guess I left it up at the lodge."

He tumbled back down the steps and went pounding off along the path.

"Tell Andrew not to bother," a voice called from inside. "I can get it when I go up for dinner."

Wanda and her mother turned in surprise. Phyllis was standing just inside the screen door, adjusting the sash of her peach-colored dressing gown. Because of the screen, Wanda couldn't see her expression clearly, though her spots seemed to have gone down.

"Oh, Phyllis, we didn't mean to wake you," Mrs. Munson said contritely. "And you certainly don't need to bother going along to the dining room tonight. I thought I'd get Pierre to bring you a tray."

"Don't be silly, Florence, my ankle feels much better. I think it's just a strain, after all, not a real sprain—and if I wear my flat sandals, or maybe those huaraches I bought in New Mexico. . . . I mean, I certainly want to add my own congratulations to Drew on catching that—that—whatever it's called. Especially since I seem to have played a part in it."

"Old Rusty," Mrs. Munson said vaguely, with a nod. "Oh, you heard all that, did you? Such a fuss about an ugly old fish—and then to throw it back after all that. . . . But how nice if Mr. Farnsworth thinks you bring him luck," she added comfortably, picking up her needlework. "Wanda, dear, would you run in and get my white sweater? Get one for yourself, too; it'll be chilly once the sun goes down. And you'd better put the terrarium away now and wash your hands, if Dad's through in the bathroom. The bell will be going soon."

Wanda was obeying the first of these injunctions when she was waylaid outside her parents' room by Phyllis, who grabbed her by the arm and pulled her down the hall into her room, shutting the door behind her.

"If you breathe one single word about what happened today—" Phyllis's eyes were large and fierce even without mascara.

"I told you I wouldn't," Wanda said, jerking her arm away.

"Because you were too embarrassed, right? Well, good, because I'll kill you if you do." Phyllis studied her for a moment. "Better yet, I'll tell everyone about how you're scared of escalators and revolving doors."

Wanda tried not to flinch. These were two babyish worries she knew she should have outgrown, never mind that she'd actually read about an escalator that started running backward, toppling people over like dominoes into a heap at the bottom, also about a woman who'd been strangled by her own scarf in a revolving door. She thought of saying in that case she'd tell everyone about the Mallomars in Phyllis's nightgown drawer, but decided against it. She might still need that in an emergency.

She said cautiously, "Then you aren't still mad at Mr. Farnsworth?"

"What do you think? Of course I'm still mad at him!" Phyllis glared at her. "And I'll find a way to pay him back, too, one of these days. Dental floss! Imagine him pawing through my bag that way, among all my personal things. . . . But since there don't seem to be any hard feelings on his part—" She shrugged. "Well, if there's one thing I've learned, it's not to argue with success. Luck! Ha!"

She turned to her closet, yanking the curtain aside so hard she almost brought down the rod, and started shoving through the hangers.

"Fishermen really do believe in luck," Wanda told her. She wondered if Gus would ever think of her as a bringer of luck. She herself was not a lucky person, having never found so much as a single four-leaf clover. But maybe this didn't matter so much when the luck was basically up to the other person.

"Right. Because they're crazy. But if a crazy, rich, unmarried fisherman decides I bring him luck, *I'd* be crazy to fight it."

Phyllis flung some dresses down on the bed and gave Wanda a belligerent stare. When Wanda didn't say anything, she said more calmly, "I guess you think that's terrible of me, don't you, Wanda? But what does a kid like you know about insecurity and bills and veins beginning to show on your hands? Not to mention gray hairs, which at least you can do something about. The only luck I care about is not tripping and breaking my leg on the way to the altar."

"No, I think it's probably smart," Wanda said thoughtfully. "I mean, as long as you don't *hate* him," she added, her conscience getting the better of her burning desire to be a flower girl at Phyllis's wedding as soon as possible.

"Only in a rowboat. The rest of the time he's not so bad—better-looking than your grandfather ever was, and richer, too. Something of a cold fish, of course."

Hearing what she'd just said, Phyllis threw back her head and laughed—the first genuine laugh Wanda had ever heard from her, full-throated and rather unpleasant. Then, catching sight of herself in the mirror, she frowned and said with a return to her usual irritable manner, "When is your father ever going to get through in the bathroom? My curling wand's in there, and just look at my hair—! For heaven's sakes, run along, Wanda, I need to change. The blue tonight, I wonder? Or maybe the beige two-piece would be better with flat shoes. . . ."

As Wanda went back out into the hall, she almost collided with her father coming out of the bathroom, freshly shaved, in a yellow sport shirt that showed off his new tan.

"Everyone just about ready for dinner?" he said loudly, then winked at Wanda and followed her into the back bedroom she shared with Andrew. "Thin walls these cabins have," he said, closing the door behind him. "Do I gather the bridge game is back on for tonight?"

Wanda nodded, rummaging in her drawer for her navy cardigan. "I guess it was never really off," she said. "At least as far as Mr. Farnsworth was concerned." She looked in the closet for her sweater and found it hanging on the hook underneath her windbreaker.

Her father looked thoughtful. "Do you know, I'd say they deserved each other," he said. "I never thought I'd say that about anyone in regard to Phyllis, but— What's the frown about?"

"I just remembered I left my beach bag over at Great Harriman."

"Well, you can get it in the morning—no one will bother it."

"Yes, but it has Rita's swim flippers in it. I shouldn't just leave them there. I mean, they're practically brand-new, and what if someone borrowed them?"

Mr. Munson sighed. "Now, Wanda, I'm sure

no one would. And even if they did, it wouldn't hurt the flippers."

"But what about little kids? That can be dangerous, you know, putting flippers on if you don't really know how to swim—they can drag you down. No, I better go over after dinner," Wanda decided. "Do we have any extra flashlight batteries? Regular ones, I mean? All I have are the little kind."

Mr. Munson looked at her helplessly. "No, but all our flashlights are working fine. I checked them before we came. Yes, yes, I know, batteries can run down"—he held up a hand—"but anyway there'll be a moon tonight."

"Unless it clouds over," Wanda said.

When the bell rang for dinner a few minutes later, Wanda was standing at the bottom of the porch steps, sniffing the air for a hint of rain and eyeing the lone cloud in the sky, a soft sunset smudge lying on the ridge above the cabin. It wasn't anywhere near where the moon would be, unless of course a big wind came up and moved it.

Her father called to her to go on; he'd be along with Phyllis in a minute. Up ahead there was a distant crunch of footsteps on gravel and the sound of voices and laughter on the still, clear air—the Hyatts and the Jacobsons, strolling toward the lodge for dinner. With a last look at the cloud, Wanda ran to catch up with Andrew and her mother.

Suddenly her step was light, her thoughts dancing and fluttering like the floating sleeves of her mother's white sweater, glimmering mothlike in the dusk ahead of her. Someday, after Phyllis was safely married to Mr. Farnsworth, she would tell Gus how she'd saved Phyllis in the woods, and all because of worrying so much. Gus would probably give her his darkest scowl; but somehow Wanda thought he might believe her.